THE HALLOWEEDS

VERONICA COSSANTELI

Chicken House

2 PALMER STREET, FROME, SOMERSET BA11 1DS

Text © Veronica Cossanteli 2016

First published in Great Britain in 2016

Chicken House

2 Palmer Street

Frome, Somerset BA11 1DS

United Kingdom

www.chickenhousebooks.com

Veronica Cossanteli has asserted her right under the Copyright, Designs
and Patents Act 1988 to be identified as the author of this work.

Cover design and interior design by Steve Wells

Illustrations by Mark Beech

Typeset by Dorchester Typesetting Group Ltd

Printed and bound in Great Britain by CPI Group (UK) Ltd, Croydon CR0 4YY

The paper used in this Chicken House book is made from wood
grown in sustainable forests.

1 3 5 7 9 10 8 6 4 2

British Library Cataloguing in Publication data available.

ISBN 978-1-910002-33-9
eISBN 978-1-910655-60-3

CHAPTER ONE

It was an ordinary, boring Wednesday afternoon.
Until, quite suddenly, it wasn't.

It's double Science on Wednesdays. Miss Drupe
showed us a film about Food Chains. It wasn't very
cheerful. This green stuff called algae got eaten by this
invisible stuff called plankton. The plankton got eaten
by a fish, the fish got eaten by a seal and then the seal
got eaten by a shark.

The seal had whiskers and big, chocolate-y eyes.
When the shark grabbed it, everyone went *Oooh!* and
Awwww! and Maisie Milligan started to cry. Nobody
bothered about the fish much, or the poor plankton.
As for the algae – well, that's how it works, isn't it?

Plants get eaten all the time, and never get a chance to eat anybody back.

Or that's what I thought.

'And now,' said Miss Drupe, when the film was over, 'you are going to make up your own food chains, and draw them in your books.'

I drew some grass, then a cow. I'm not brilliant at art; my cow looked more like a Labrador. I borrowed Maisie's pink gel pen and gave it a strawberry-scented udder, to make it more cow-like. What eats cows? I drew a stick man. What eats people? I chewed the end of my pencil. Lions? Tigers? Zombies? Tyrannosaurus Rex?

I had just decided on a crocodile (I can draw them) and was reaching for the green pen when the classroom door opened and Mr Stilton, the head teacher, stalked in.

Mr Stilton has a face like a disappointed sheep. He nodded at Miss Drupe, then peered at us all over the top of his glasses.

'Dandelion?' he said. 'Dandelion Bone?'

A few people giggled. They always do. I looked down at my science book.

'Dan?' said Miss Drupe. 'Day-dreaming again, I suppose. *Dan!*'

There are two Dans in our class. One of them is Daniel Roberts. *His* parents didn't ruin his life by naming him Dandelion. The other one is me.

I asked Dad, once, why they'd done it.

'It's tradition. All the eldest sons in our family are called Dandelion. They always have been. It's my name too,' he pointed out. 'It never did me any harm.'

'Really?' I didn't believe it. 'Are you telling me that you never got teased? Not *ever*?'

'Well, maybe a bit,' he admitted. 'Well, maybe quite a lot. But it wasn't all because of my name. It was the whole being-a-nerd thing. Beetles and stuff. You know.'

I did know. My parents are Entomologists, which is the posh word for being Totally and Ridiculously Obsessed with Insects. Insects matter more to them than anything else in the world – and that includes their children. My sister Martha complains when the Parasitic Fig Wasp gets more attention than she does. The Grub's still a baby and hasn't realized yet that it's less important than the Madagascan Hissing Cockroach. I'm the eldest, so I've had longest to get used to it.

It might have been confusing, Dad and I having the same name, but we managed. We cut it up into fractions: I was Dan; he was Lion. (My grandfather was Del. Dan-Del-Lion.) Dad's third of the name didn't really suit him. He wasn't very lion-ish. Glasses, knobbly knees, and his favourite food was cauliflower cheese. But he was Dad, and he was OK. So was Mum.

Which is why it came as a bit of a shock when Mr Stilton took me to his office and told me that they had both been eaten by cannibals.

I had never been in the Head Teacher's office before. You only go if you're really good or really bad. I'm never *really* anything: I'm just me. It was a musty, mud-coloured room, with old school photos on the walls and a very large desk. In front of the desk, rocking on her chair and chewing bubble gum, was my sister Martha. She had a witch's hat on her head, made out of black paper and sticky tape; Year 4 were getting ready for Halloween.

Mrs Butters was there too. Mrs Butters is the Teaching Assistant in Martha's class. She's a kind lady who gives you plasters when you fall over, even if you're not bleeding. Martha says she smiles too much. (Martha's fussy about people.) She wasn't smiling now. She was blowing her nose into a paper tissue.

'Sit down, Dandelion,' said Mr Stilton.

I waited for him to say something to Martha about the chair-rocking and chewing – they're both against school rules – but he didn't. Martha hardly ever gets told off. It's because she's small for her age and looks like a meerkat.

Mr Stilton sat down opposite us. He gave a little

cough and straightened some papers, looking more like a sheep than ever: a sheep who has just discovered what mint sauce is for. Out in the playground, Mr Clench was barking at Year 3 to line up at the end of their PE lesson. A fly buzzed against the window. A clock ticked on the wall, ticking away the last minute of my life – my life as it had been for a whole eleven years, and never would be again.

Then he told us about our parents. And the cannibals.

Nobody said anything for quite a long time – unless you count Mrs Butters, sniffing into her tissue. I could hear my heart beating; the rest of me seemed to have stopped working. My brain had jammed, like a computer when it freezes.

It was Martha who broke the silence. 'Do cannibals eat you raw? Or cooked?'

We all looked at her. Mrs Butters made a noise like a trodden-on cat.

'What?' said Martha crossly. 'It's not like it's *true*!'

Mr Stilton cleared his throat. 'I'm afraid that there is . . . evidence. As I understand it, your parents' expedition had taken them a long way into the rainforest – further than most people go . . .'

'They're looking – they *were* looking – for the Greater-Spotted Giant Purple One-Horned Dung

Beetle,' I said. My voice had a wobble in it; it didn't sound like me. 'It's very rare. Nobody's seen it for over a hundred years.'

Mr Stilton shuffled his papers. 'Your parents became separated from their guides; nobody knows how, or why. Trackers were sent out to search for them but all they found was ... this.'

Sliding something out of a brown envelope, he pushed it across the desk towards us. It was a photograph of two people holding hands. Or rather – what was left of two people, which wasn't very much. The hands and a bit of arm, about halfway up to the elbow ... I could see a man's wedding ring, and a SpongeBob SquarePants watch – just like the one we had given Dad for Christmas. The other hand was wearing a silver ring with a tiny blue scarab beetle set in it, like the one Mum always, always wore ...

I felt hot, then cold. Then a bit sick. Martha had stopped chewing.

Mr Stilton gave another of his little coughs. 'The young lady who looks after you—'

'She's not a young lady,' said Martha. 'She's Caramel.'

'... is on her way to pick you up. You need to collect all your belongings,' Mr Stilton went on, 'as you are unlikely to be coming back to this school. You will be going to live with your aunt and uncle.'

'But,' I said, 'we don't have any aunts or uncles.'

Mr Stilton frowned and looked down at his papers. 'It says here – Lady Grusilla Bone, Daundelyon Hall, Witches' Cross.'

'Oh,' I said. 'Her. She's not exactly an aunt. More of a *great*-aunt. Or even a great-great-aunt. We've never met her.'

'I'm not going to live with someone I've never met,' stated Martha. 'I might not like her.'

'She might not like us,' I said.

'I'm not going.' Martha was definite. 'You can't make me.'

A week later we were on a train, heading for Daundelyon Hall – and Great-Aunt Grusilla.

The train was crowded. Caramel pushed Martha and me into seats opposite two old ladies. 'I won't be far away,' she told us. 'I'll be sitting over there, with the Grub. Dan, look after Martha.'

'Don't you dare even *try*!' hissed Martha, as we squeezed into our seats. She started arranging her dinosaurs so they could see out of the window. Martha's not really the sort of sister you *can* look after without getting a kick, or a stegosaurus thrown at your head.

Caramel made her way down the carriage and sat in the only seat left, next to a young man with a bushy ginger beard, brightly coloured arms and a tarantula tattooed on his neck. Caramel looked him up and down and offered him a chocolate.

Caramel believed in chocolate; she also believed in charms to keep away bad luck. Chocolate and charms: she liked to have plenty of both with her at all times. Her chocolate was stashed in bags and pockets and under her pillow; her good luck was inked on her skin. Her arms and legs and back were a rainbow swirl of horseshoes and shamrocks and sugar skulls and charms against the Evil Eye.

'We can't be too careful, in my family,' she'd explained. 'Things happen to us – more than they do to other people. We choke on fish bones and get struck by lightning and trampled by mad cows. My gran would never get out of bed on a Friday the thirteenth, she was so afraid of bad things happening. Until one Friday the thirteenth the bedroom ceiling fell down on her. My Auntie Melba got towed away in a portable toilet. My cousin Candy got stuck in a lift and missed her own wedding. Then there was the business of Uncle Roly and his false teeth . . . but we don't talk about *that*: it was too dreadful. All I can tell you is that there was a very *large* amount of blood.'

It was Dad who had chosen Caramel to look after us while he and Mum were away looking for the Greater-

Spotted Giant Purple One-horned Dung Beetle. All sorts of people had applied for the job. They all said how much they loved children – you could tell that they hadn't met Martha.

Mum wasn't totally sure about Caramel. I think it was the motorbike and the bristly hair that put her off – but Dad said she was perfect. 'She can't help it,' he'd said, 'with a name like Caramel Lovejoy.'

It hurt, thinking about Mum and Dad. As I sat squashed in my corner, staring out of the train window at the trees and hedges and fields whooshing by, the top of my nose prickled. I had to blink, to stop the world turning wet and blurry. The two old ladies opposite were eating sandwiches and drinking tea out of a thermos flask. I think they must have noticed the blinking because they started smiling at me in a kind, sympathetic sort of way. *That's all we need*, I thought gloomily. I glanced at Martha, who was reading her book: *A History of Famous Murderers Through the Ages*. Martha isn't good with kind old ladies.

One of them rustled about a bit in her bag and brought out a packet of rich tea biscuits. 'Would you like one, ducks?'

'No, thank you.' I smiled back, as politely as I could.

Then, of course, they had to offer one to Martha. Martha looked up from *Famous Murderers* and stared suspiciously at the rich tea biscuit.

'No, thank you,' she said, at last. 'I don't take biscuits from strangers. I can't tell if they've been poisoned.'

The old lady looked a bit startled but said she could tell Martha was a very sensible little girl. Martha frowned. She hates it when people call her little.

The journey seemed to go on for ever. Towns and stations came and went. The old ladies got off without saying goodbye. I didn't blame them. A mother and her toddler sat down in their place, then some giggling teenage girls, then a businessman in a suit who disappeared behind his newspaper. Down the carriage, I could see the Grub snoozing on Caramel's lap while she and the man with the ginger beard admired each other's nose piercings.

Diddly-dee, diddly-doop. Martha had put down her book and was playing her favourite game: *Rob-it Rabbit and the Attack of the Carrot-Monster. Diddly-dee, diddly-doop, diddly diddly diddly* . . . Until, at last, she ran out of lives. *Diddly DOOP DOOP DOOP!*

'Stupid rabbit,' said Martha. 'Who cares?'

I tried to read my book but mostly just stared out of the window. We had started the journey in sunshine; now rain was streaking the glass. The drops were all travelling backwards. I wanted to go backwards too –

back in time to Before Cannibals. The businessman was still rustling his paper. I looked at the headlines: some royal person was going to have a baby; somebody had thrown an egg at the Prime Minister; an Indian rhinoceros had gone missing from a wildlife park; a footballer had crashed his Ferrari into a tree; heavy rain and flooding expected...

Finally the speaker crackled.

Our next station stop will be Witches' Cross, in approximately two minutes' time. Passengers are reminded to take all their personal belongings with them. Please mind the gap between the train and the platform...

Down the carriage, Caramel was rising to her feet, causing a small avalanche of chocolate wrappers. We were there.

CHAPTER TWO

Witches' Cross Station was deserted. There was nobody on either of the platforms, a sign on the Ticket Office window said *Closed Until Further Notice* and the car park was empty.

'Now what happens?' I asked. 'How do we get to Daundelyon Hall?'

'Your aunt said there'd be somebody to meet us.' Caramel shifted her grip on the grumbling Grub. 'They're probably stuck in traffic.'

'What traffic? There isn't any,' I pointed out. 'There isn't even a proper road.'

There were no houses, either. Just a bumpy lane, leading into the middle of nowhere.

'It's getting dark,' said Martha. 'I don't like this place. I want to go home.'

'Sssshh!' Caramel hushed us, with a finger to her lips. 'Can't you hear it?'

Clip-clop, clip-clop . . .

A minute or two later, four ink-black horses trotted briskly into the car park, with a coach rattling behind them.

'Whoa!' The driver was small and wizened, like an ancient, wrinkled monkey. As he dragged on the reins, the horses pulled up to a snorting, stamping stop. The old man peered down at Martha, holding her dinosaurs, at Caramel, holding the squirming Grub, and at our pile of suitcases. Then he looked at me, and touched his cloth cap. 'That you, Master Dandelion?'

I blinked up at him. 'Er – I'm Dan, yes.'

'Best get going then, while the 'osses can still see the road.' The old man jerked his head at the sky. 'Don't want to be driving through the Deepness by moonlight. What with the wolufs and such.'

'Wolufs . . . There are *wolves*?' I wasn't sure I believed him.

'All manner of beasts in the Deepness.' Hopping down from his seat, he began heaving our suitcases into the coach. 'Wolufs. Hoonicorns.'

'Unicorns?' Martha believes anything. 'Really?'

Not really. I didn't say it out loud; I didn't want to be rude.

'Wild porkers too,' added the coachman. 'With tusks that could rip a man apart. There'd be hunting parties up at the Hall, once upon a time. Lords and ladies left and right in those days, all so grand. Me and the dogs under the table, gnawing at the bones. I had teeth in my head, back then.' He licked his tortoise-gums regretfully. ''Tis playing with Nature, to make a man live longer than his teeth.'

Without warning, he suddenly grabbed at my hand, catching it in his own skinny claws and making me jump. His nails were grimy with earth and there was just a stump where his little finger should have been. Since seeing the photograph in Mr Stilton's office, I'd been a bit sensitive about missing body parts. I tried to pull away, but he held on.

'Good stock,' he said, pinching my fingers. 'Full of sap. A fresh green sprout, ready for the planting. You'll be putting down roots at the Hall before you know it, Master Dandelion.'

Was he trying to be funny – or was he just plain crazy? Either way, I wished he'd let go.

Martha was stroking the horses' noses. 'What are their names?' she wanted to know.

'Midnight. Ebony. Raven. That one there's Death,' said the old man. 'Watch your fingers, miss. He's high-strung. Gets uppity.'

Martha reached up to pat the glossy black neck. 'When I go to the riding stables they make me ride this fat little pony called Muffin. I'd rather ride Death. Can I sit up there, next to you, and hold the reins?'

'Room for one more up front.' He dropped my hand at last. Relieved, I put it in my pocket. I wondered if his lost finger was the result of Death getting uppity. 'T'others will have to travel inside,' he added. 'Only old Bessie Fleaspoon in there. You can sit atop of her, Master Dandelion. She won't mind.'

'I feel like Cinderella,' remarked Caramel, as he lowered the steps for her. 'Or the Queen.'

There was a gold crest on the coach door: a lion and a unicorn, both showing their teeth, reared up on either side of two crossed swords and something that looked a bit like a cabbage. Inside, there was no sign of Bessie Fleaspoon, just a long wooden box. I bumped my knee on one of its brass handles. What sort of box needed that many handles? It had six sides, two of them much longer than the others. That made it an Irregular Hexagon: we'd done those in Maths. There was only one thing I could think of that came in that particular sort of irregular hexagon . . . I shrank back, away from it, but it was too late.

'Mind yourself, Master Dandelion,' said the old man and slammed the coach door shut behind me.

I knew where Bessie Fleaspoon was, and why she wouldn't mind if we sat on her.

Bessie Fleaspoon was past minding about anything. She was in her coffin.

'Gee up! Get on!'

Martha had got her own way, as usual: the old man had given her the reins. A whip cracked the air and the horses shot forwards, bouncing Caramel and me off the inside walls of the coach.

'Easy does it, miss,' warned the coachman. "Er Ladyship'll have my guts for garters if I don't get Master Dandelion to the Hall, safe and sound and soon-as-maybe.'

Martha wasn't listening. 'Faster!' she ordered the horses. 'The wolufs are coming!'

'There aren't any wolves,' I said to Caramel. 'Are there?'

'You know Martha.' Caramel was busy with the Grub, who was trying to eat its own socks. 'She likes life to be exciting.'

Life can be *too* exciting. The thing about a boring life is that your parents don't get eaten by cannibals and you don't end up driving through wolf-infested forests, sitting on a dead body.

'Whoa!'

There was a whinny and a sudden lurch as the horses swerved. I slid sideways, almost into Caramel's lap, while she made a grab for the Grub who'd gone flying up to the ceiling. 'What was *that*?'

I peered out of the window. We were at a crossroads with nothing to see but grey boulders squatting here and there, and a single tree with spiky, blackened branches stretching out to an empty sky.

''Tis the Hanging Tree,' muttered the old man, ''Tis where they'd string up the witches. They'd leave'em a-dangling, while the crows picked their bones shiny-clean. The 'osses still jink at it; they smell the ghosts. You can hear 'em, wailing...'

'It's the wind,' said Caramel, but I saw her twisting the blue beads with the little eyes painted on them that she wore around her wrist. 'They stopped hanging witches ages ago.'

''Twere All Hallows' Eve, the last one,' wheezed the coachman. 'In 1699. Leastways, they *meant* to hang her. Slippery as eels, witches: wriggle through your fingers. Soon after, tree were struck by lightning. Witches' fire, folks said. Slow down, missy, and keep your eyes on the road. We'll have 'er Ladyship mad as a bag of ferrets if

Master Dandelion ends up in the ditch. They want him up at the Hall in one piece. For now.'

Clip-a-clop clop. Clip-a-clop clop. The coach swayed from side to side as the horses cantered on and on, further and further into the middle of nowhere. Caramel winced every time the wheels went over a bump. The Grub was red-faced and roaring. Coffins are not the most comfortable thing to sit on.

'We're there!' cried Martha at last. 'Dan, look – it's a *castle*!'

I slid off the coffin and knelt by the window, peering out into the twilight.

We had left the road and were clattering over a rickety wooden bridge. Ahead, hunched on a lumpy little island in the middle of a river, was Daundelyon Hall. The old castle had mostly fallen down, leaving part of the old walls, and the gatehouse with its drawbridge and spiked portcullis to keep enemies out. One tall tower was still standing, wearing what was left of its battlements like a broken crown, ancient and mossy, with little flowering weeds growing out of the stones. You could see where old Bones had added bits and pieces of their own until the Hall grew up, higgledy-piggledy, out of the castle ruins. The only thing that looked modern was the fancy gold lettering cut into the stone above the arch of the portcullis:

FISHBLOOD AND BONE
FUNERAL DIRECTORS

Underneath, in smaller letters, it said:

SPECIAL OFFER
BURY ONE, GET ONE FREE

Just what we need to make us feel better, I thought dismally. *Living in a Funeral Home.* At least it explained Bessie Fleaspoon: she wasn't just some random dead person who had come along for the ride. Caramel didn't look too happy. She was fiddling with her beads again.

'Aieee!' We both jumped and Caramel swallowed a scream as a dark shape swooped suddenly out of nowhere, beating against the window of the coach, blotting out the light. Wings whirred; a black beak stabbed at the glass – *ttt ttt ttt.* The glint of a bright eye – then it was gone.

'Was that a magpie?' Caramel sounded flustered. '*One for sorrow . . .*'

I shook my head. 'I think it was a crow.'

Waaark! Waaark! Whatever it was, it was following the coach.

'A bird tapping on a window . . . that's bad news.'

Caramel was upset. 'It's an omen.'

As we swept through the castle gatehouse, the coach gave another lurch. My nose slammed against the window; the Grub bellowed and Caramel shut her eyes tight.

'*Whoooo!*' Martha was squealing with excitement.

'Easy now,' the old man cautioned her. 'You'll have us all over. Watch out for them stones. Roof's a-tumblin'. Walls a-tumblin'. If much more comes down, we'll be a-sittin' on a pile of rubble.'

When we clattered to a halt, I wasn't sorry to say goodbye to Bessie Fleaspoon and get out. Martha had already bounced down from her perch, all bubbly and pleased with herself because the old man had told her she was 'a natural' with the horses. People are always telling Martha how clever she is. It was a matter of time, I reckoned, before her head got so big it exploded.

Between tall stone pillars, the Hall's heavy wooden doors stood open. On one side, a stone unicorn reared up; on the other, a snarling lion. Cut into the lintel was an inscription. Time and weather had rubbed away at it, but you could still make out the words:

Lion-toothed, sharp of claw,
Bones rule, ever more.
Here lives and breathes a true-born Bone,
Or these walls crumble, stone by stone.

It looked as if quite a bit of crumbling had happened already. One of the pillars was cracked through, several of the upstairs windows had diamond panes missing and a number of slates seemed to have slid off the roof and landed in the courtyard. Behind the tumbledown chimneys, a domed glass roof rose up, mottled green like a dirty fishbowl.

Footsteps sounded, and a woman's voice rang out bossily. 'Is he here?'

'Aye, my lady,' replied the coachman. 'Young Master Dandelion and the little miss. And the big miss and a little squeaking wriggler too. More of the gatehouse's come down,' he added. 'Grazed a wheel, coming through. 'Osses don't like it. Wreck and ruin, we're comin' to. Ruin and wreck.'

'Fiddlesticks!' The voice had an edge to it, like glass splinters or uncooked gooseberries. 'Not any more. Now the boy is here, all will be well. Where is he? *Bring me the Heir!*'

'Aye, m'lady.' The old man gave me a shove between the shoulder blades and I fell, sprawling, into the shadows of Daundelyon Hall.

The floor was cold stone; the walls were dark panelled wood, hung with swords and shields, daggers and axes. Empty coffins stood propped against beams. A cannon crouched in a corner, next to a pile of cannonballs the size of Christmas puddings. The grandfather clock in one corner had stopped, its hands at ten to three. Hanging in between the weapons, long-dead Bones stared down their oil-painted noses. Not a single one of them was smiling. They all had their lips squashed together as if they were trying not to burp.

'Why did nobody tell them to say *cheesy pizza*?' whispered Martha behind me.

I picked myself up, my nose wrinkling. The smell made me think of dead things: dead roses, old grass clippings, the rotting rat Dad had found in the shed last winter. At the foot of a grand staircase, in between two suits of armour, stood Great-Aunt Grusilla.

It's rude to stare – but sometimes you just can't help it. Large and square, Aunt Grusilla was squeezed into a dress with wide skirts that reached all the way down to the floor – like a hippopotamus done up in someone's best lace curtains. Jewels sparkled at her throat and wrists and dripped from her ears. Her hair was milky yellow, like smoked haddock. Dotted with pearls and little bows, it was piled high on top of her head around a glass fishbowl, with real fish swimming in it. She clasped a small black and white dog with bulging eyes and bat-like, hairy ears. 'At last!' Flinging open her arms, she dropped the dog – it landed on the stone floor with a *splat* and a whimper – and came sailing towards us. 'Dearest boy!' she cried, completely ignoring Martha. 'At last – you have arrived!'

As she folded me in her arms, the stones in her necklace scratching my cheek, I was nearly suffocated by the smell of compost. If I rolled my eyes upwards, I could see her chins wobbling above me. Her face powder silted up her wrinkles and clung to her moustache hairs, as if somebody had dressed up a walrus.

She squeezed me even tighter. 'Daundelyon Hall has been waiting for you! Welcome home!'

'This is not our home,' stated Martha, behind me. 'We live at number thirty-two, Shakespeare Road.'

Above my head, Aunt Grusilla flared her nostrils like a horse; I could see all the way up her nose. 'In my day,' she said coldly, 'little girls were seen and not heard.'

'In the Stone Age,' muttered Martha, under her breath.

Luckily, at that moment the clang of a gong rang out, the sound swirling around us.

'That will be Pokiss,' said Aunt Grusilla. 'We don't get many visitors here. Not live ones. She's very excited.'

The person who came shuffling through a doorway towards us didn't *look* terribly excited. She was dressed in a man's pinstriped suit, several sizes too big, fluffy slippers and a woolly bobble hat, out of which poked strands of cobwebby hair. Her pink-rimmed eyes were the colour of dirty dishwater. She had no eyelashes, no eyebrows, and her skin was the colour of pale cheese.

'Here he is, Pokiss.' Aunt Grusilla swung me round. 'Daundelyon Hall has a new Bone. Behold the Heir!'

'Heir-y fairy, looks contrary,' said the person in the pinstripe suit, unimpressed. She looked me and Martha up and down. 'Pygmies,' she said.

'They are *children*,' Aunt Grusilla corrected her. 'Poor little orphans, with nobody to look after them. So they have come to live with us. Isn't that delightful?'

I winced; her rings were digging into me. As I glanced down at her fingers gripping my shoulders, I felt a little ripple of shock: one of them wasn't there. Just a stump – just like the old man's. Was that Death being uppity again? I was going to stay well away from those horses . . .

'Ssss.' Pokiss sniffed. A drip of moisture wobbled at the end of her nose.

'We do have somebody to look after us,' said Martha. 'We have Caramel.'

Caramel had been helping the coachman unload our luggage from the coach. As she stepped through the doors, the Grub grumpy and grumbling in her arms, Aunt Grusilla and Pokiss stared at her studded biker jacket, silver piercings and spiked hair. You could see she had made a special effort today, with black lipstick and her best dangly bat earrings.

'Hedgepig,' said Pokiss. 'Ssspiky. Not nice-sss.'

'She *is* nice,' argued Martha. 'She reads us stories and makes chocolate pudding and has beautiful tattoos. Look at me – I'm a vampire!' Climbing into one of the upright coffins, she crossed her arms over her chest and closed her eyes. Martha likes to be the centre of attention.

'Doesn't fit.' Pokiss whisked a tape measure out of her jacket pocket and began measuring Martha – up and down, and across the shoulders. 'Pygmies need itssssy-bitssssy boxes. Not this one. Too big. Might fit the Hedgepig.' Now she was measuring Caramel, who clutched at her beads, rolling her eyes like a spooked dog.

'Stop measuring our guests, Pokiss,' chided Aunt Grusilla. 'They are not here to be fitted for their coffins. You must be polite and take their coats. Then we can show them to their rooms.'

Pokiss gave another sniff and held out her bony hands.

'*Oh!*' I said, without meaning to, and had to turn it into a pretend cough, trying not to stare at her fingers – all eight and a half of them.

Not another one? The residents of Daundelyon Hall

did seem to have a great many accidents – or rather, they seemed to have all had exactly the *same* accident. Except that Pokiss wasn't only missing a little finger, but half the ring finger on her other hand too.

Caramel peeled off her jacket. Underneath it she was wearing a sleeveless top. Pokiss stepped backwards, hissing like a startled snake. Her eyes were fixed on the bright blue Eye tattooed on Caramel's shoulder.

'Caramel's charmed all over,' explained Martha. 'That one keeps her safe from the Evil Eye and bad magic.' She had walked all the way around Aunt Grusilla, inspecting her hair. 'What happens to the little fish,' she wanted to know, 'if you bend over?'

'A lady never bends over,' stated Aunt Grusilla. 'It is unbecoming, uncomfortable and unnecessary. Where's Lambkin?' She looked around for her little dog, who was cowering behind one of the suits of armour. 'Come along, Dandelion. I shall show you the Heir's Bedroom.'

CHAPTER THREE

We followed Aunt Grusilla up the wide curve of the staircase, with its polished banisters, and along a gallery full of more paintings of long-ago Bones. I stopped by a picture of a man wearing an old-fashioned wig, white and curly like judges wear, with a heavy gold coat, white stockings and buckled shoes. He had a long nose and a dreamy look in his eyes and made me think of Dad. In fact, all the men in the paintings reminded me of Dad. You could tell by their clothes that they had lived in different centuries, but their faces were the same. Mum said I'd look like Dad myself, when I grew up: it's the Bone Family Resemblance. I don't mind the face; I'm not so happy about the bald patch.

In the largest frame of all, dark and spotted with age, was a lady with bright gold hair and very red lips, her flesh all pink and pillowy.

'That was painted soon after my marriage.' Aunt Grusilla heaved a gusty sigh. 'I was considered a Great Beauty in my youth. Men fought each other for my affections. One of them even wrote a poem comparing me to a Greek goddess.'

'Quite a fat goddess,' remarked Martha, inspecting the painting. 'Full of Greek food, I should think.'

'Did Great-Uncle Dandelion fight for you?' I asked, as Aunt Grusilla gave Martha a nasty look.

'He didn't have to. I knew it was my destiny to be mistress of Daundelyon Hall – then, now and always.' She stopped, so suddenly that I almost bumped into her, and flung open a heavy wooden door. 'The Heir's bedroom,' she announced. 'Dandelion, this will be yours.'

The walls were dark red, patterned with the same gold crest as I'd seen on the coach door: the lion and the unicorn, with the crossed swords and the plant. Blood-red velvet curtains hung around a massive four-poster bed.

'Who's *that*?' Martha had elbowed me out of the way for a better look.

A giant figure in chainmail armour stood at the foot of the bed. One metal-gloved hand held a sword. The other brandished what looked like an iron football chained to a stick. It was studded all over with fearsome-looking spikes, sharp enough to split your skull and burst your brains.

'Sir Lyon de Beaune,' said Aunt Grusilla. 'Your ancestor. He came over from Normandy with William the Conqueror in 1066 and fought at the Battle of Hastings. The sword was one of his favourites. He had two: the other one was buried with him.' She stroked the iron blade with her ringed fingers. 'It was known as the Lion's Tooth. You were named after it, Dandelion.'

'No, he wasn't – he was named after a weed.' Martha giggled. 'With little fluffy yellow flowers.'

'I was *not*! I was named after Dad. And his dad.'

'And his father, and his father before him,' agreed Aunt Grusilla. 'Just like your Uncle Dandelion. You were all named after Sir Lyon's swords. The *Dents de Lyon*. The Teeth of the Lion.' She touched the spiked iron ball. 'And this was Sir Lyon's flail: the Lion's Paw. You can see him in the tapestry.'

She gestured at the strip of fraying cloth, stained the colour of weak tea, which stretched nearly all the way around the room. It was designed like a comic strip: hundreds of little men with pointy shoes and egg-shaped helmets, some of them on horseback, were hurling spears and shooting arrows, doing their best to kill each other.

'There's Sir Lyon, fighting the English.' Aunt Grusilla pointed at a figure, taller than any of the rest. Sir Lyon had one Englishman skewered on his sword, like a kebab, while he bashed another over the head with the Lion's Paw.

'Nice,' said Martha, who likes a good fight.

'The tapestry was stitched by Sir Lyon's wife, Lady Clotilda,' Aunt Grusilla informed us. 'It was her life's work. As you can see' – she pointed to where the last picture ended in half a horse – 'she died just before it was completed.'

'Of boredom, I expect,' said Martha. 'I hate sewing.'

Aunt Grusilla looped back the moth-nibbled curtains hanging around the four-poster. 'The chamber pot under the bed was used by King Charles I, shortly before his head was cut off. It is a room full of history and tradition.'

I looked at Robo-Ancestor, waving his Lion's Tooth and Lion's Paw, and thought I'd swap history and tradition, any day, for my bedroom at home.

'Twenty-five to ten.' Martha was peering at a grand silver clock. 'That's wrong.'

'It's stopped,' I said. 'Like the one downstairs.'

'A good thing too,' said Aunt Grusilla sharply. 'I won't have all that *tick-tock tick-tock*ing: Time galloping along, pleasing itself. In this house, it must do as it's told.'

In the room next door to mine, Martha's four-poster bed was smaller and not quite so grand. On the wall hung a tapestry of a pale lady in a pale gown, sitting in flower-speckled grass. Beside her a unicorn knelt, resting its head in her lap.

'That is Lady Clotilda, taming a unicorn,' Aunt Grusilla informed us. 'Unicorns can only be tamed by an innocent maiden, gentle and virtuous. When she was a girl, Lady Clotilda caught one, here in these woods. She wove that tapestry herself to prove it.'

'It's not exactly *proof*,' I said. 'It's a picture, made of thread. It's not like a photograph, is it?'

'There are unicorns in the Deepness to this day,' said Aunt Grusilla, ignoring me.

'Where will Caramel sleep?' asked Martha. 'And the Grub?'

Aunt Grusilla looked down her nose at the Grub. 'Does it squeal?' she asked, pinching its arm. The Grub stared at her, then let out a yell. 'I thought so,' nodded Aunt Grusilla. 'I had an infant myself. It made the same noise. It had to live in the attic, until it was old enough to know better. Pokiss will make a bed for you up there,' she informed Caramel. 'If the rats and the bats are a nuisance, she'll lend you a musket.'

'What happened to your squealing baby?' Martha wanted to know. 'Where is it now?'

'Long gone,' snapped Aunt Grusilla. 'The ungrateful creature ran away. Good riddance to her!'

Martha would have asked more questions – she's nosy – but at that moment the gong crashed, making us all jump.

'Dinner,' announced Aunt Grusilla. 'Come along. Pokiss doesn't like to be kept waiting.'

As we followed her back down the stairs, we passed the old man staggering the other way, lugging our suitcases. Aunt Grusilla stopped, one hand on the banister rail.

'Is everything ready for the funeral tomorrow, Boy? You've made the usual . . . arrangements?'

'Coffin's snug in the coach, m'lady.' The old man stared down at his feet. 'Just have to pretty up the 'osses in the morning.'

'Hurry up with that luggage, then, and get back to the Glass House,' commanded Aunt Grusilla. 'I shall be making an inspection soon and I want to see those plants standing up straight. I won't allow any drooping.'

The old man touched his cap and carried on, puffing and wheezing up the stairs.

'In the old days your uncle and I had a great many servants,' explained Aunt Grusilla. 'Now it is just Pokiss and Boy. Pokiss is coffin-maker, chief undertaker, lady's maid and cook. Boy looks after the horses, drives the funeral coach and tends the garden. He's slow on his feet and his wits have curdled, but he does have a way with plants. We have some very rare and valuable botanical specimens growing in the Glass House. There was an Unfortunate Incident recently and one of them died, but everything will be all right now.' She ruffled my hair, making it flop into my eyes. 'Now that you're here, Dandelion. Our very special boy.'

I don't like having my hair messed with. I don't like being called *special*. I don't like being called Dandelion, even if does mean Lion's Tooth. Behind Aunt Grusilla's back, I pulled a face at Martha. She pulled one back. But I couldn't help noticing that she looked just the tiniest bit jealous.

Pokiss served dinner with a flowery apron wrapped around her pinstripe suit. Nobody spoke much. We were too far apart: the dining-room table was the length of a swimming pool. Aunt Grusilla sat at one end, with Lambkin at her feet. I sat halfway down. If I peered around a silver bowl full of white lilies, I could see Martha sitting opposite. The bowl had the same crest on it as the coach and my bedroom walls: the lion and the unicorn, the swords and the cabbage, with the words *Semper virens* written underneath. It was on the plates and the napkins, too.

'That lion looks as if it's about to sick up a hairball,' remarked Martha.

'That is the Bone Crest,' Aunt Grusilla told her coldly. 'The Bone Lion and Lady Clotilda's unicorn, with the family motto: *Ever Green*.'

'If you ask me, the unicorn's got colic,' said Martha, unimpressed. 'Where is Great-Uncle Dandelion?' she asked, as Pokiss ladled something brown and runny into her bowl. 'Isn't he hungry?'

'Your uncle is old and in poor health,' said Aunt Grusilla. 'He has his own rooms in the tower and must not be disturbed. That part of the house is out of bounds; you are to keep away. Any excitement would be dangerous. He is in a very delicate condition.'

Martha frowned down at her bowl. 'What is this?'

'Kitten Noodle Ssssoup,' said Pokiss.

There was a silence. Everyone put their spoons down, except for Aunt Grusilla, who was slurping noisily. 'Eat up,' she told us, 'or there'll be no pudding.'

I stared into the greasy depths, stirring it round and round the bowl, letting it trickle off my spoon. The noodles weren't too bad. They slid, worm-like, down my throat and made the bowl look emptier. Pokiss had shuffled back into the kitchen. Aunt Grusilla was still slurping. I was the only person who noticed Martha pour her soup into the lilies. Further down the table, Caramel was pretending to sip from her spoon, letting it dribble down the Grub's bib.

'Whoops,' I said, dropping my spoon. Ducking under the table to pick it up, I took my soup bowl with me. 'Pssst! Lambkin!'

The little dog pricked up his feathery ears and came pattering towards me. I straightened up, with an empty bowl, just as Pokiss came back in with the pudding.

'Jelly,' she announced, planting something grey and wobbly in front of me.

'Very nourishing,' said Aunt Grusilla. 'Eat up, or you'll hurt Pokiss's feelings. She spent all morning boiling the bones.'

What seemed like much, much later, we all sat huddled on Martha's bed with the curtains drawn around us like a tent, eating bananas and chocolate. The Grub was asleep, rolled up in a blanket, too little to be homesick.

'We'll have to run away.' Martha was wrapped in Mum's old blue cardigan. It came down to her knees and smelt of Mum. She had squeezed it into her suitcase when nobody was looking. 'Let's go back home. We don't need Great-Aunt Gorilla. Caramel can look after us.'

'I wouldn't be allowed,' said Caramel. 'Your aunt's your Legal Guardian. And you shouldn't call her that, Martha.'

'No,' agreed Martha, 'because I like gorillas. They're lovely. Aunt Grusilla's *not*. She has furry eyebrows. Why's her hair up in the air like that? And why does she dress like someone out of history? She *smells* like someone out of history too. Dead mouse-ish. We'll have to hide, and never be seen again, like Aunt Grusilla's daughter. I bet she ran away because she couldn't stand the food.'

'Or being shut in the attic, with the rats.' Just as I said the word 'rats', we heard the noise, somewhere above our heads.

Tck-tck-tck. Tck-tck-tck-tck. A pause, then it came again. *Tck-tck-tck-tck. Tck-tck-tck.*

Martha hugged Mum's cardigan more tightly around her. '*I'm* not scared of rats,' she declared. 'But the dinosaurs might be – if it was a great big huge one with yellow teeth and a baldy tail.'

Caramel was twisting her beads. 'That's not a rat.' She bit her lip. 'It's the Deathwatch Beetle! It's a sign, a bad omen. It means a death in the house.'

'Whose death?' demanded Martha.

'Yours,' I told her, 'if beetles chew through that beam. The ceiling will fall on you, like it did on Caramel's gran. The whole place is falling down. Didn't you read what it said above the door? *The walls will crumble stone by stone.*'

'No, they won't,' argued Martha. 'It said there had to be a *true-born Bone* in the house and there is. Not Great-Aunt Gruesome – she wasn't born a Bone; she just married one – but that still leaves four of us: Uncle Dandelion, you, me and the Grub. Uncle Dandelion's the oldest; if anyone's going to die, it should be him.'

'It doesn't happen like that,' I told her. 'It's not like everyone queues up and waits for their turn. Although – Aunt Grusilla did say Uncle Dandelion wasn't very well.'

'I bet he's fine,' said Martha. 'He just stays in his tower so he doesn't have to eat Pokiss's food. I bet he gets Chinese takeaways delivered through a secret passage. He's probably stuffing himself on pancake rolls and special fried rice right now.'

I wished she'd shut up about pancake rolls. My stomach was rumbling. 'I wonder if there *are* any secret passages,' I said, to take my mind off it. 'It's a very old house. There might be.'

We had finished the chocolate. Caramel had

smoothed out the wrapper and was folding it into the shape of a little purple bird.

'It's a duck,' said Martha.

Caramel shook her head. 'It's a crane. In China and Japan cranes mean good luck and long life – and that's what we're all going to have,' she said firmly. 'Tomorrow, I'll ask your aunt about my bike.' Caramel loved her motorbike. It couldn't be left behind at 32 Shakespeare Road, so she'd sent it ahead, in a van. 'It must be here, somewhere. I'll ride to the shops in the morning and get some proper food. We'll be all right – as long as we don't have to live off Pokiss's cooking.'

Martha snuggled up to her. 'You won't leave us, will you, Caramel?'

'Of course not, silly.' Caramel gave her a quick hug. 'I'm not going anywhere. I promise.'

CHAPTER FOUR

The next morning, Caramel wasn't there.

'Wake up.' Somebody was shaking me. My nose twitched. Something smelt flowery, familiar.

Mum?

I opened my eyes. Martha, still wearing Mum's cardigan over her nightdress. 'Wake *up*!'

The little spark of happy feeling inside me fizzled and went out. I squeezed my eyes shut again. It had taken me ages to get to sleep. I'd pulled the curtains around the bed, shutting out the suit of armour. I had the feeling Sir Lyon de Beaune's ghost was only waiting for me to fall asleep before he smooshed my brains all over the pillow with his Lion's Paw. Invisible

Robo-Ancestor turned out to be worse – as long as I had my eyes fixed on him, he couldn't move – so I'd drawn the curtains back again.

Ant. Bedbug. Cricket. Dung beetle. Earwig. Firefly. Grasshopper. Hawkmoth. Some people count sheep, if they can't sleep. If your parents are entomologists, you count insects instead. What began with 'I'? I must have fallen asleep, still trying to remember.

'Ichneumon wasp,' I mumbled now. 'Iris borer.'

'Dan, wake up. Wake up *properly*.' Martha was pummelling me. 'Caramel's gone. I've looked and she isn't *anywhere*.'

'What?' My bleary brain began to clear. 'What time is it?'

'Nobody's up yet. Not even the Grub. I went up to Caramel's room to see if she was awake and she's *gone*!'

'She can't have gone very far. She's probably in the bathroom.' I yawned. 'Hey, stop it – what are you doing?'

Martha was tugging the covers off me. 'You have to come and *see*.'

'The people in these paintings all look the same,' I complained, as we padded through the corridors past the family portraits. 'Even the dogs all look like Lambkin.'

Martha wasn't in the mood to care. She raced ahead

of me, up the back staircase that led to the attics and the musty, dusty little bedroom Caramel was sharing with the Grub. The window was small, high and dirty. A fat spider hung in it, well-fed on flies. The Grub was asleep in its cot, bunched up like a caterpillar in its green sleepsuit. Caramel's 'bed' was just a mattress pushed up against the sloping wall. The stained sheet and ragged blanket Pokiss had given her lay flat, neatly tucked. You could tell that no one had slept under them.

'She probably just switched bedrooms,' I whispered, so as not to wake the Grub. 'I don't blame her: the roof leaks.' I pointed at the damp stain on the pillow. 'The rain's getting in.'

Martha shook her head. 'She wouldn't leave the Grub. Anyway, I've looked. She's nowhere.'

Grey early morning light trickled in through the tiny square of window. A fly buzzed against the glass, dangerously close to the spider's web. The window catch was stiff, as if it hadn't been used for a very long time, but a bit of wiggling got it open and the fly looped away. We were at the back of the house; the window looked out over gravel paths and bushes clipped to look like toadstools and peacocks and chesspieces, towards the domed roof of a very grand building. Its high walls were made of glass, set into a skeleton of white iron. It was nothing like the rickety greenhouse Dad used for messing about with flowerpots in at home. You could have fitted the whole of 32 Shakespeare Road inside this.

Beyond it was a maze: the sort you can walk through, between tall hedges, and get lost in. With my bird's-eye view, I could see all the way to the centre. While Martha banged drawers open and shut, I tried to work out the way through. Just as I thought I'd solved it, a movement caught my eye.

In the middle of the maze, an oddly dressed person in a three-cornered hat and tall boots had appeared out of nowhere. There was a flash of blue and gold; a large bird skimmed the top of the hedges and landed on his shoulder.

I blinked. 'Martha – there's somebody out there.' I forgot about whispering. 'Dressed as a pirate. With a parrot and everything.'

Martha wasn't listening. 'Meatballs! All Caramel's stuff's gone!' She slammed the last drawer shut. 'There isn't even any chocolate. And where are her Lucky Things?'

I turned away from the window. This was serious. In case the charms inked on her skin weren't enough to keep her safe, Caramel liked to have backup: a used horseshoe, the smiling cat with the waving paw, a sprig of gypsy heather, a stone with a hole in it, her lucky crystals, an acorn in case of lightning strikes and a string of garlic in case of vampires. We'd watched her arrange them last night; now they were nowhere to be seen.

'That Poke-Hiss person has taken them!' Martha was furious.

'We don't *know* that,' I said.

'Yes, we do,' argued Martha. 'You saw her face when she saw Caramel's magic Eye. It was like it had stung her. Dan, what have they done with Caramel?'

I wished I knew. There was a grizzling sound coming from the cot. The Grub was awake. I leant over the bars and sniffed. I looked at Martha.

'Uh-uh. No way.' She shook her head so hard her hair flew across her face. 'I'm not changing it. You're the eldest. You do it.'

Sometimes babies smell; sometimes they don't. I wasn't an expert on what had to happen in between. Before Caramel, it was mostly Dad who took care of all that. Mum, who went to work at the museum every day, said it was a pity humans weren't more like insects. Mother insects lay their eggs on a big pile of something good to eat (a leaf, some rotting meat, maybe a pile of poo – sometimes even another insect), then move on; their babies hatch out and look after themselves.

As I struggled with poppers and cotton wool and

squirming, unhelpful Grub, I had a thought. As soon as I'd had it, I wanted it to go away, but it wouldn't. 'The thing is,' I said, reaching for the bottle of bottom-cleaner, 'we're not Caramel's *family*. We're her job. She gets paid to look after us. At least, she did. But if Aunt Grusilla and Uncle Dandelion don't want to pay her, she'll have to find a different job.'

Martha stared at me. 'Why?'

I shrugged. 'Grown-ups have to have jobs. They need money.'

'What does Caramel need money for?'

'Well . . . chocolate.' Obviously. 'And she's always paying to get her bike fixed . . .'

'Her bike!' Martha clapped her hands. 'She wouldn't go anywhere without *that*. It's like her pet. We have to find it. If the bike's still here – so's Caramel! Come on, let's go and look!'

'Wait . . .' But she was gone. I could hear her footsteps, along the passage and down the creaking stairs.

Gathering up the Grub, I took one last look out of the window towards the maze. It was empty. Something crunched under my bare foot. It was one of Caramel's blue beads, painted with the lucky eye. I bent and picked it up.

By the time I caught up with Martha, she was already

at the Hall's front doors, twisting the heavy brass handles.

'Meatballs! The stupid things won't open.' She gave them a kick.

'They can't,' I pointed out. 'Look. Bolts.'

The bottom bolt was easy. The top one was out of reach. 'You'll have to give me a piggy-back,' said Martha.

I dumped the Grub in a nearby coffin and braced myself as she leapt for my shoulders. 'Ouch – you're heavy!'

'I still can't reach. You'll have to stand on tiptoe. You're too short, Dan. Can't you grow?'

'You're the one who's small for her age,' I said crossly. '*You* grow.'

'Stop wobbling about,' ordered Martha. 'I can't do anything if you *wobble*.'

'*Tssss . . .*'

I felt cold breath on my cheek. Spinning around, I lost my balance. 'Owwwch!' We crashed to the floor in a tangle of arms and legs.

Pokiss stood over us, wearing a pair of men's striped pyjamas. My nose was centimetres away from her feet. I stared at them – I couldn't help it. She had no toenails. Just soft slug-sausages, peeping out from the end of her fluffy slippers.

'Is it burglars, Pokiss?' Aunt Grusilla's voice boomed

out from the gallery above. In a long nightgown, with a bonnet tied under her chin, she hovered above us like a large white cloud.

'Not burglars. Pygmies. Essssscaping,' said Pokiss.

'Where's Caramel?' demanded Martha. 'What have you done with her?'

'Are you talking about that very peculiar nursemaid?' enquired Aunt Grusilla. 'She's gone. She left rather suddenly, didn't she, Pokiss? It's for the best. A strange creature – not a proper person to be in charge of children.'

'She *was* proper!' said Martha furiously. 'Properer than you!' I could sense one of her Fusses boiling up inside her, like water in a kettle. Martha's Fusses are legendary. She doesn't cry: she shouts and stamps, and makes the walls shake. Which is why she usually ends up getting her own way. 'It's not for the best – it's for the *worst*!' She was yelling now, and pounding on the door. 'Let me out! I want to go home – I want *Caramel*!'

'Pokiss is going to count to ten,' said Aunt Grusilla coldly. 'If you're still making that noise by the time she's finished, you will be sent to your room. Deal with her, Pokiss; she's giving me a headache.' And she billowed away, Lambkin yapping at her heels.

'One, two, eight, nine, *ten*,' cheated Pokiss. Grabbing

Martha by the ear, she marched her, kicking and yelling, up the stairs. 'Pygmy squealing loud enough to rattle the Bones and wake the dead. *Tssss . . .*' It sounded like air escaping from a puncture. Pokiss was laughing. 'You don't want to do that. Not here . . .'

Disturbed by the fuss, the Grub had shuffled to the end of its coffin and was holding out its arms, hopefully, to the nearest suit of armour.

'No use asking *him*.' I looked at the axe gleaming in the metal hand and scooped the Grub out of reach. 'He won't be any help.'

Upstairs, I could hear Martha crashing around in her bedroom, kicking the furniture and screaming for Caramel. Pokiss was outside her door, dropping the key into her pyjama pocket and looking like somebody who has just trapped an especially annoying mosquito in a glass jar and doesn't mean to let it out again.

'Heiry-fairy,' she said, when she saw me.

I didn't want to talk to her but I was hungry and, with Caramel gone, worried about food. 'What happens about breakfast?'

'Porridge happens,' said Pokiss unhelpfully. 'But not if you're late.'

When the gong crashed, half an hour later, I was dressed. Martha had gone quiet so I knocked on her door. There was no answer, so I squinted through the keyhole.

'Are you all right?'

'Go away,' growled Martha's voice, so I hoisted up the Grub and went downstairs for breakfast.

The lilies in the dining room were dead; I guessed they hadn't enjoyed Martha's soup at supper. Aunt Grusilla sat at the head of the table, inspecting her reflection in a silver-handled mirror. Pokiss stood behind her, with a comb and a mouthful of pins, sticking an arrangement of forks and silver teaspoons into her hair, topped off by a bunch of peacock feathers.

'Dandelion!' Aunt Grusilla waved the mirror at me. 'I am finishing my toilette. You may make yourself useful.' She held out a small jewelled box.

I opened the lid and stared down at the little strips of fur, lying in rows like tinned anchovies.

'Pokiss makes my eyebrows for me. Out of mouse fur. Pretty, aren't they?' said Aunt Grusilla. 'You may choose me a pair – make sure that they match.' She made me hold the mirror for her, while she glued them on. 'Now, my rouge, Pokiss.'

'Lively today,' Pokiss remarked, pushing a bowl towards her. It was full of tiny beetles crawling over each other, trying to climb up the sides.

'Not for long,' said Aunt Grusilla, picking up a heavy

marble pestle.

'Oh, don't!' I exclaimed. 'The poor things . . .'

But it was too late. The beetles had already been ground into a red paste and Aunt Grusilla was smearing them on to her jowly cheeks with what looked like a dead rabbit's foot. 'There,' she said, admiring the results in her mirror. 'What do you think, Dandelion?'

I opened my mouth, then shut it again. I couldn't think of anything to say.

'Cat's got his tongue,' sniffed Pokiss.

'When I was a young woman,' said Aunt Grusilla dreamily, 'men were *often* tongue-tied by my great beauty. Words failed them. Sit down and eat your breakfast, Dandelion. Pokiss will take care of the Infant.'

But when Pokiss stretched out her eight and a half skinny fingers, the Grub clung to me and I held on to it, tight.

'I'm looking after it. It and Martha. I told Mum and Dad that I would. I promised.'

Take care of them, won't you, Dan? Promise me . . . I could still hear Mum's voice. We'd been saying goodbye at the airport, under the sign that says DEPARTURES.

I'd promised without thinking. How hard could it be? Mum and Dad were only going to be away for a few weeks and, to be honest, I'd expected Caramel to do most of the looking-after. I had NOT expected cannibals – or Caramel to disappear into thin air. Just for a moment, I felt almost angry: *I'm eleven; what am I meant to do?* Most of the time, not even Mum and Dad could get Martha to behave. And what did I know about bringing up babies? The only thing I'd ever looked after, all by myself, was a stick insect. But a promise is a promise.

I swallowed, and looked Aunt Grusilla in the eye. 'A Bone keeps his word.'

'I hope you're not going to be stubborn.' Aunt Grusilla was frowning. 'Like your parents were. It didn't do *them* any good. They should have paid attention when I told them I wanted to adopt you.'

'Adopt me?' I stared at her. 'What for?'

'For Daundelyon Hall, of course. The Hall must have an Heir. I offered them money, jewels, whatever they wanted. Your mother had the chance to swap you for a very nice diamond tiara, worth a queen's ransom. Stupid woman – she said that nothing in the world would make her part with any of you.'

She was wrong about that, I thought. *The cannibals made her part with us.* But it was nice that she'd said it.

'I don't think entomologists wear tiaras much,' I said, as Pokiss plonked a bowl down in front of me, full of something that looked like wallpaper glue with raisins in it. Some of the raisins had wings. One of them was still buzzing. I picked it up with my spoon and put it on the edge of my bowl. It cleaned itself up and flew away.

Aunt Grusilla was shovelling up fly sludge when she gave a sudden angry grunt, fishing something black and spiky out of her bowl.

'My eyelashes keep falling off, Pokiss!' she complained. 'These spider-legs are useless.'

'Should have left them on the ssspiders,' muttered Pokiss. 'Legs is legs; lashes is lashes. Ssshouldn't go mixing them up. Stick on what you like – you can't turn a frog back into a tadpole.'

'Humdudgeon!' snapped Aunt Grusilla. 'You can do anything you want, if you try hard enough. Dandelion, come here and hold the mirror for me.'

As she was sticking her spider lashes back on, using dabs of leftover porridge for glue, Pokiss cleared my bowl away, still half-full.

'You don't seem to have much of an appetite,' Aunt Grusilla complained. 'He won't grow big and strong if he doesn't eat, will he, Pokiss?'

'Or even if he does. Tssss . . .' Pokiss was leaking air, laughing again.

'Fresh air and exercise,' decided Aunt Grusilla. 'That's what he needs. We must have you in the best possible health, Dandelion. Not long to wait now.'

'Wait for what?'

'All Hallows' Eve.' Pokiss had grabbed at my hand and was pinching my fingers, in the same way as Boy had done. Her touch was cold and snaily and made my skin prickle. I jerked my hand away.

'Halloween?' With a stab of homesickness, I thought of other Halloweens, of going trick-or-treating with Chris and Ryan who lived at number 29. Last year, Mum had made us take Martha. She'd made a massive Fuss over her witch's costume. We'd hardly got to the end of the road before she tripped over her broomstick and fell over. To be fair, she didn't cry but we couldn't stop her nose bleeding. So as not to waste it, Ryan had 'borrowed' some of her blood for his zombie costume. We ended up with more sweets than ever before. Somehow, I didn't think this year was going to be as much fun . . .

'Run along and play outside,' ordered Aunt Grusilla. 'Don't cross the drawbridge and you are *not* to go near the Glass House.'

'What about Martha?' I asked.

'Fresh air is dangerous for girls: they should be kept pale and delicate,' said Aunt Grusilla. 'Your sister may remain in her room and reflect upon her Failings.'

I didn't think Martha was reflecting on her Failings.

I was pretty sure she was reading *Famous Murderers* or on the next level of *Rob-it, Rabbit* by now. But I didn't say so.

I'd meant to knock on Martha's door again, but it turned out that I hadn't done up the Grub's nappy properly and it had sort of exploded. By the time I'd sorted it out, I found Pokiss squatting, like an evil spider, on a low wooden stool outside Martha's bedroom. A candle flickered beside her, burnt down nearly to its saucer. Head bent, she was whispering to herself, fingers busy as she fiddled with a lump of wax, squashing and squeezing it into the shape of a small, pale person ...

I saw her pull a pincushion from her apron pocket.

'*Tssss* ...' A pin flashed silver as she drove it into the wax doll's leg.

I stared at the doll, then at Pokiss.

Voodoo?

'Ow!' came Martha's voice from behind the door.

Pokiss stared back, her watery eyes not blinking. Anger whooshed through me.

'Stop it!' I ordered her. 'Leave my sister alone!'

Digging in my own pocket, I found Caramel's blue bead and held it up between my finger and thumb.

'*Tsss* ...' As the air leaked out of Pokiss, she seemed

to shrink. The pincushion dropped from her fingers. I pounced, snatching it up, then backed away down the corridor, holding the bead in front of me like a weapon until I was around the corner and out of sight. Then – I admit it – I turned and ran.

CHAPTER FIVE

I put the Grub into its buggy and wheeled it around the side of the Hall. My head was full of what had just happened. Martha must have bumped into something, I decided, just as Pokiss stuck the pin in. Coincidence, that was all. No one believed in voodoo. I was still holding the pincushion: just a ball of cloth, stitched into the shape of an ugly little head with bristly pin-hair and staring button eyes. With a shiver, I stuffed it into my pocket.

Without thinking about it, I had arrived at the entrance to the maze. Could I get to the middle? And, if I did, would I find any trace of the mysterious stranger in the three-cornered hat?

I tried to remember the route I'd worked out from the attic window. *Turn left. Second right. First right. Second left.* Or was it second right, first left? I couldn't remember. The overgrown hedges to either side were dark and unfriendly, squeezing in on us, slapping at us with their branches and shutting out the light. The Grub was whimpering, kicking out its fat legs and pulling at its buggy strap. It gave me an excuse to give up and turn around before I got us both hopelessly lost.

'Come on,' I said. 'Let's go and look at the portcullis.'

Parking the buggy in the arch of the gatehouse, I stood staring up at the blackened metal teeth hanging over us. How long was it since they had last come crashing down to keep the Hall safe from its enemies?

'Wouldn't stand there. Not if I were you.'

Boy was on the drawbridge, clutching a little bunch of wild flowers. He was dressed in a shabby black suit and a top hat. The hat was too big and had slipped down over one eye. It looked slightly squashed, as if somebody might once have sat on it.

'Does it still work?' I asked, looking up at the portcullis.

'Spear you like a pea on a fork, if it has a mind to.' The old man made a slicing movement with his hand. Several petals fell off his posy.

I took a step backwards, out of reach of those teeth, and nearly fell off the drawbridge.

'Don't want to do that, neither.' Boy blinked his tortoise eyes at me. 'River's high and wild, frothing like a mad dog. Rain since Michaelmas and more to come. 'Tis a sign, when the cows point their tails to the east. River will rise; dungeon will flood.'

'There's a *dungeon*?' I looked back at the Hall. 'Where?'

But the old man just shook his head. 'River gets in,' was all he'd say. 'Washes the bones white as snow.' He clutched at my wrist suddenly, making me jump. He was looking at my watch. Mum and Dad had given it to me for my eleventh birthday: it was waterproof, with an alarm and a stopwatch and a light and a button that told you the time on the other side of the world. Pushing back his hat, Boy bent over my wrist, tilting it this way and that.

'Eh, lookee . . .' he mumbled. 'A little, little clock to wear on a man's arm. What will they be thinkin' of next?' He gave me a suspicious look, as if it might be a trick. 'It tells you the time, if you ask it?'

I nodded. 'Ten fifty-three. See?'

Boy straightened up, drawing in a sharp breath. 'Bessie's funeral! Time to make the 'osses pretty.'

I didn't want to hang about under those metal teeth,

but before turning to follow Boy, I threw away Pokiss's pincushion. With one last look at those evil button eyes, I hurled it into the water, watching the rings of ripples as it sank. I know you shouldn't throw things into rivers – it's not fair on the fish – but I didn't want it in my pocket; it was making my skin prickle.

I caught up with Boy in the stable block, where Midnight, Ebony, Raven and Death were stamping in their loose boxes.

Perched on a hay bale, I watched him brush the horses until they shone, crooning to them as he combed their manes and tails. Then the bridles went on, with their funeral plumes of black feathers.

'They look smart,' I said.

'Aye, Bessie'd like that.' As Death snorted, making his plumes nod, Boy patted his silken black neck and let out a wheezy sigh. 'Time's a slippery fish. Doesn't seem more than a blink since she were no bigger than that sister of yours. Where is the little miss today?'

'In her room,' I told him. 'She's not allowed out.'

'Like that, is it?' He shot me a sharp, sideways look. 'It used to be the same with the other little lass, back in the old days. Miss Jacobina.'

'Aunt Grusilla's daughter?' I thought of the little girl who had been sent to live in the attic, to teach her not to cry. 'What happened to her?'

'Not a soul as knows.' Digging in his pockets, Boy found a sugar lump and gave it to Raven. Jealous, Death nudged jealously at the old man's hat, knocking it to the ground. Picking it up, Boy brushed the hay off and hung it on a nail. 'They didn't let her out of doors much. I'd see her little flower face, up at the attic window, pale as a daisy. Then one day she'd gone – upped and bolted in the night. Eh, well – all in the past now. Can't stand around tongue-wagging. Bessie has to get to church on time.'

He was leading Midnight and Ebony out to the waiting coach when a sudden loud *waa-ark* and a wingbeat made us all jump. A big black bird flapped past, skimming the roof of the coach before spiralling upwards to land on the battlements of the old tower. The horses whinnied, hooves ringing.

'Nasty flappy thing,' grumbled Boy, hanging on to Midnight's head collar. 'Always following the coffins. Pick your bones as soon as look at you! No respect for the dead.'

I looked up at the ruined battlements, then at the heap of rubble on the ground below. 'The tower's falling down,' I said. 'The whole house is.'

'Nay.' Boy sounded like one of his own horses. 'Not any more. *Here lives and breathes a true-born Bone, Or these walls crumble, stone by stone,*' he recited. 'Stones'll stay where they are, now the Heir's here.'

'Me?' I wasn't sure about being responsible for holding a whole house up. 'But there's been a *true-born Bone* here all the time. What about Uncle Dandelion?'

'That weren't my fault!' Boy sounded upset. 'I'm not allowed to tell – don't ask me to, Master Dandelion – but it were never my fault! 'Er Ladyship says it was – but it were the pudding what done it.'

'What pudding?' I was confused. '*What* wasn't your fault?'

Boy clicked his tongue at Death, who was trying to eat Raven's funeral plumes. 'Naughty, greedy Cabbage,' he muttered. 'And now the rest of 'em are fuss-potting: droopin' and floppin' and flingin' their leaves on the floor. I know what they're hungering for. I raised them from cuttings; they're like my own flesh and blood. I know what they want, but I won't give it 'em – no matter what 'er Ladyship says.'

I couldn't help thinking that maybe Aunt Grusilla was right: Boy's wits really had curdled. I remembered science lessons, and Miss Drupe's food chains. Plants were always at the bottom. The cabbage got eaten by the snail; the snail got eaten by the bird; the bird got eaten by the cat; the cat got eaten by . . . I remembered the Kitten Noodle Soup and felt a bit sick.

Boy laid his little bunch of flowers on top of the

coffin, then hopped up into the driving seat. 'No hat,' he muttered, patting the top of his head. 'That won't do.'

'I'll get it,' I offered.

The top hat was hanging from its nail, where Boy had put it. A grey cat had appeared out of nowhere and was lazily scratching its flea bites in an empty loose box. Behind it, a pitchfork rested against the wall, next to a mound of hay. When the cat saw me looking, it stood up and stalked away. I didn't see where it went; my eyes were fixed on the hay. I'd seen the glint of shiny red metal. Was that a handlebar poking out? And, now I looked properly, wasn't that the trace of a tyre track on the floor? I could feel my heart beating and the cold tingle of my skin.

They hadn't done a very good job of hiding it.

It was Caramel's motorbike!

'What's happened to Caramel? Where is she?'

Boy was reaching down for his hat but I wasn't letting go of it – not until he gave me an answer.

'Her bike's in there. She wouldn't have gone anywhere without it. Where is she?'

Boy's eyes slid away from mine. The horses sidled as his gnarled hand twitched on the reins. 'I'm just an old man,' he mumbled. 'Old as tombstones, with a head full of moss and thistledown: what do I know? Give me my hat now, Master Dandelion,' he pleaded, 'or we'll have poor Bessie late for her own funeral.'

It was no use: I'd never get any sense out of him. I let go of the hat. Jamming it on his head, Boy gave the reins a shake and the horses plunged forwards.

I had to tell Martha about the bike. If Pokiss was still guarding her room, I'd write a note and slide it under her door.

But there was no sign of Pokiss – or of Martha. The door stood wide open; her bedroom was empty.

'Martha?' I looked in my own room, but she wasn't there either. Racing down the corridor, I took the stairs to the attic.

'Martha? *Martha?*'

Bouncing in my arms, the Grub thought we were playing a game and squealed with laughter.

'Not funny,' I panted. Couldn't it feel the hammering of my heart? 'Where *is* she?'

I searched every cobwebby corner of the attic but, just like Caramel, Martha wasn't anywhere. *You stupid idiot.* I told myself off. *Why did you leave her alone with Pokiss? You promised you'd look after her. You PROMISED.*

Back down the stairs and along the corridor, I flung open every door I came to, slamming it shut again when Martha wasn't in there – until I kicked open a door and found Aunt Grusilla.

'Really, Dandelion!' She looked down her nose at me, disapproving. 'A gentleman *never* bursts in on a lady when she is embroidering her smalls!' She was sitting in a chair by the window, holding a threaded needle, with something white and frilly stretched across the wooden frame on her lap. 'The Bone Crest,' announced Aunt Grusilla, holding up her embroidery for me to admire. 'It is very dear to my heart. I like to keep it close.'

I looked at the snarling lion, the crossed swords and the cabbage, and the half-finished unicorn. It wasn't her *heart* they were going to be close to. She was stitching them on to her knickers. And 'smalls' wasn't at all the right word: they were enormous.

'Where's Martha!' I said breathlessly. 'What have you done with her?'

'The girl?' Aunt Grusilla jabbed the needle into her knickers. 'Pokiss has taken her into the Deepness.'

'Into the *woods*?' I must have pinched the Grub, gripping it too tightly; it let out a squawk.

'If she wants to stay at Daundelyon Hall, she needs to make herself useful.' Aunt Grusilla yanked her thread tight. 'She needs to catch me a unicorn.'

I opened my mouth, then shut it again. It's an odd feeling when, one by one, the grown-ups around you all turn out to be crazy . . . 'Why?' was all I could think of to say. 'What do you want a unicorn for?'

'Dung,' said Aunt Grusilla.

'Dung?' I blinked at her. 'You mean . . . like poo?'

'For the plants,' explained Aunt Grusilla. 'Our *special* plants in the Glass House. They are sickly – a bad case of the weevils, we fear, gnawing at their roots. Pokiss has looked it up in her Book. Their only hope is unicorn dung.'

Dad had once ordered a pile of manure for his roses. Mum had given us all clothes pegs to wear on our noses. But that had come from horses.

'Are you sure,' I asked, 'that Pokiss is reading the right book?'

Aunt Grusilla frowned. 'In my day, Dandelion, children did not argue with their elders and betters.'

'I'm not *arguing* exactly,' I said. 'But you said unicorns can only be caught by gentle, innocent maidens . . .'

'Pure and virtuous,' agreed Aunt Grusilla. 'Everyone knows that.'

'Right,' I said. 'And you've sent . . . Martha?'

Aunt Grusilla pressed her lips together and put another stitch in her knickers. 'She is not the well-behaved girl I'd hoped for,' she admitted. 'I blame your parents: not enough discipline and too much getting her own way.'

I'd often thought the same thing; that didn't mean I liked Aunt Grusilla saying it. 'If Mum and Dad let Martha get away with stuff sometimes it was only because they loved her!' I said furiously. 'What's wrong with that?'

Aunt Grusilla gave me a scornful look. 'Love! A most unhelpful feeling, always getting in the way of Common Sense. I won't have it in the house.' Little Lambkin yelped under her skirts as she gave him a kick to prove it.

'Please,' I begged. 'You can't leave Martha in the woods all alone. She'll get lost.'

'Not if she's tied to a tree, she won't,' said Aunt Grusilla. 'Pokiss took plenty of rope.'

'Supposing she gets eaten by wolves?'

'That,' snapped Aunt Grusilla, 'would be very tiresome and inconvenient of her. We shall have to risk it. I want that unicorn.'

'Just supposing,' I said, 'that there *isn't* a unicorn . . .'

'Fiddlesticks,' said Aunt Grusilla briskly. 'Of course there's a unicorn. People have seen it – a white beast. And Pokiss found hoof prints. If your sister can't catch it, she's no use to me. The wolves can have her, or Pokiss will find a Home for Unsatisfactory Children we can send her to. Somewhere a long way away: Timbuktoo, or the North Pole.'

'You can't *do* that!' I said desperately.

'I'm her Legal Guardian.' Aunt Grusilla bit off her thread. 'I can do what I like.'

It was no use – and I needed to get away from Aunt Grusilla before I ended up puncturing her with her own embroidery needle – so I shut the door on her (as loudly as I could) and stamped back to Martha's room. The Grub was making my arms ache by now, so I put it on the floor and sat down on Martha's bed. *Famous Murderers* was lying open on her pillow, under a jumble of plastic dinosaurs. I held the triceratops on my lap, stroking its beaky nose. Martha had thrown it at me so often the point of one of its horns had snapped off, but she loved it just the same.

'Don't worry,' I told it. 'Nothing bad will happen to her; I won't let it. I said I'd look after her – and I shall.'

By the time the gong clanged, I'd decided to go into the Deepness myself. I'd look for Martha and bring her back.

But first I had to get through lunch.

'Toad.' Pokiss slammed a plate down in front of me. 'In-the-hole, where it belongs. Not hopping about where it doesn't.'

It looked more like *frog*: skinny little legs with

webbed feet sticking up as if the poor thing had dived, headfirst, into the batter. I picked around the legs, but it's hard to get full on just Hole. When nobody was looking I slipped my frog to Lambkin under the table. This turned out to be a mistake: he sicked it straight up again, all over Aunt Grusilla's feet. She aimed a kick at him, and went off to change her vomity shoes.

Pokiss cleaned up the mess. When she noticed the bits of chewed frog in it, she gave me a hard, suspicious look. I said the Grub needed changing and escaped back up to the attic.

I opened a jar of baby food: Cheesy Pasta Delight. Usually Martha and I agree that it looks like snot; today, I was hungry enough to reckon it looked quite good. When the Grub had finished, I licked the spoon and scraped out the jar.

The Grub was rubbing its eyes and moaning. It was used to having a nap after lunch. I bundled it into its cot and pulled the string on its musical mouse. Three rounds of *Twinkle, Twinkle, Little Star* and its eyes had closed. It would sleep for at least an hour. Surely that was long enough for me to find Martha and get back again? I crept out and headed for the stairs – and the woods.

Nobody stopped me. Aunt Grusilla must have gone back to embroidering her knickers; Pokiss was either clearing up lunch or concocting something horrible to give us for supper. The stables were empty: Boy and the horses weren't back from Bessie Fleaspoon's funeral. It was easy to slip, unseen, through the gatehouse, across the drawbridge and in between the trees.

CHAPTER SIX

Only a very stupid person goes crashing into a wood – the sort that has no paths – and doesn't mark the way they've come. It was a pity I didn't realize that sooner. After about twenty minutes of blundering about, I had no idea where I'd come from, or where I was going. I was scratched and bleeding from pushing through branches, and all the old fairy tales Dad used to read to us were rushing through my head. Witches' cottages; murdering queens; hungry wolves: bad stuff happens in woods. The silence pressed in around me; all I could hear was my own breathing.

'Martha!' I yelled. 'Martha!'

Nothing. Then:

'*Spaghetti Bolognese,*' said a voice above my head.

'Who's there?' Staring upwards, I thought I saw a glimpse of blue and gold. Leaves rustled, a twig snapped and suddenly I was struggling in the folds of a net. Losing my balance, I toppled over. 'Owww*mmph!*'

What started as a shout of alarm ended with me getting a mouthful of rotting leaf litter. As I lay there, squirming like a maggot, a figure dropped lightly out of the tree, landing with a black-booted foot either side of my ribs. The face looking down at me was in shadow, a three-cornered hat tipped low over the nose. It was the person I'd seen in the maze, still in his pirate costume.

'*Macaroni, minestrone!*' The parrot came swooping down to land on his shoulder. '*Sushi, noodles, apple strudels . . .*' It dipped its head up and down, cackling with laughter.

'Looks like I've netted a shrimp,' said the pirate gruffly. 'What were you doing, shrimp, floundering about in Black Jack's waters?'

I spat out an acorn. 'They're not *your* waters. They're not even *waters*. Get this thing *off* me!'

'A squawking shrimp. It makes more noise than you do,' remarked the pirate to the parrot. Turning his back on me, he swung himself back into the tree he'd dropped out of.

'Hey!' I shouted, but there was no answer. I was lying there alone, wrapped tight, like a sausage in its skin. *This is how a fly feels*, I thought, *when it's caught by a spider*.

My feet began to lift off the ground. Feet, knees, bum, shoulders . . . I was dangling, head down. All my blood was running into my skull – any minute now my brain would burst – and the rope that had tightened around my ankles was biting into my skin.

I was being hoisted up through the branches. Leaves fluttered against my face; twigs cracked and scratched. I could see the ground through the mesh of the net, getting further and further away. At last, the upward pull slackened off. I hung there, turning in slow circles, to the right, to the left.

'See you the other end,' said Black Jack. 'I *think* you'll clear the rail, but I can't be sure so you might want to curl up a bit. I don't want your brains splattered all over my deck, thank you very much.'

I felt a shove and a jolt, heard the whirr of a zip wire above my head; then I was bucketing through the air, downwards and sideways, the world a blur as startled pigeons clattered up from the branches all around me. Alarmed by the idea of splattered brains, I tried to make myself as small as possible. It was a relief when I jerked to a stop, without slamming into anything.

Through the whirling dizziness, an ivy-twined wooden railing swam in front of my eyes – I must have whizzed over it with about a centimetre to spare. Below me were bare, scrubbed boards. I don't know how long I swung there: long enough to make me very glad that I hadn't eaten much lunch. Pokiss's cooking was depressing enough the first time – you didn't want to meet it again coming up the other way.

There was a whoosh of air and a splash of blue and gold as the parrot came out of nowhere, making the net rock wildly as it clung on with beak and claws. Turning itself neatly upside down, as if to get a better look at me, it edged closer to my face. I could see the zebra stripes around its yellow eye and the black tongue in the curved beak.

'*Crepes Suzette!*' it said, not very politely. '*Tartiflette. Grosse crevette.*'

The three-cornered hat appeared, from somewhere below us. *This person has* serious *pirate issues*, I decided, looking at the frayed eyepatch and curling black moustache. Then I noticed his hands, gripping the rail in black velvet fingerless gloves. One of the finger holes was empty. Aunt Grusilla, Pokiss, Boy . . . this made four of them. They could not all have had exactly the same accident. Which meant . . . what?

He had swung himself over and was standing, hands on hips, inspecting me; my nose was on a level with his high black boots.

'Should we untangle it?' he asked the parrot, as it flapped to his shoulder. 'It looks a bit green. I don't want shrimp-sick all over my deck.'

The net jerked as he fiddled with the knots, then I was falling. As I landed with a thud on the wooden boards, he bent over me, unravelling the web of ropes. A final nudge, from the toe of his boot, and I rolled free.

'You'd better not try anything,' he warned me, 'or you'll go overboard. It's a long way down and there may not be sharks, but there are other things.'

He needn't have bothered with the threats. I couldn't even tell which way was up and which was down any more, let alone try to escape. I lay on my back, gasping like a fish, listening to the blood rushing in my ears. Where was I?

High up – I could tell that much: it was all treetops and sky. The nearest tree had no branches, no leaves, just a smooth, straight pillar of wood, stretching upwards, with a rectangle of cloth rippling out from it, puffed by the wind. I blinked. Not a tree: a ship's mast, flying a flag.

A black flag, with a white skull grinning down at me.

'It would serve you right,' said Black Jack, 'if I made you walk the plank. Why were you creeping around, spying?'

'I wasn't spying.' I sat up to defend myself. 'And as for *creeping around*, what were you doing in the maze this morning? I was watching you from the window, up in the attic.'

'You're from Daundelyon Hall?' His voice was sharp.

I nodded. 'I came out to look for my sister. Aunt Grusilla's tied her to a tree. She wants her to catch a unicorn. You don't have to tell me that there aren't any – I know that.'

'Aunt?' Black Jack's one eye was fixed on me. 'Did you say *Aunt . . .*?'

'Yes, but only because she married my — *ow!*'

He was lifting me by the collar, half choking me, staring at my face. 'Sliced sea slugs and barrels of blood – why didn't I see it before?' he muttered, letting go of me.

I flumped back down on to the deck, holding my squashed throat. A swirl of wind brought a drift of red-gold leaves. Raindrops were dotting the deck.

'*Zuppa Inglese*,' said the parrot gloomily, shaking out its feathers. '*Lemon drizzle.*'

Jack glanced up at the sky, which had turned the colour of a purple bruise. 'You'd better come below.'

Opening a hatch in the deck, he jerked his head at me.

I hesitated, not sure I wanted to be swallowed up by a pirate ship – even one parked in a tree – but the parrot was nipping at my ankles.

'OK, *OK*.' I hopped out of reach of its beak.

Below decks was dark and splintery. I hit my head on a hanging lantern, tripped over a coil of rope and crashed into a barrel marked GUNPOWDER.

'*Dampfnudel*,' said the parrot, rudely.

Jack swung down after us. With the parrot waddling behind me, cutting off my escape, I followed him past a cannon, its nose poking out of a porthole, a little galley full of cooking pots and a row of hammocks. The ship's timbers creaked, buffeted by the wind. By the time Jack pushed open a door marked *Captain's Cabin*, I was beginning to feel slightly seasick.

The captain's cabin smelt of popcorn. The floor was a map of the world: faded blue oceans full of looping sea monsters and triangular mountains marked *Here be Dragons*. The ceiling was painted with stars. In-between was mostly taken up by the oak tree growing in through the open porthole. Its branches were looped with strings of shells and pearls and coloured stones, sparkling blue and green like seawater in sunshine. I forgot about being seasick and alone in a fancy-dressed lunatic's lair, deep in the woods where nobody would hear me scream . . .

'It's beautiful,' I said. 'But why are there so many *fish*?'

There were whole shoals of them, little wooden ones, each one different, dangling on bits of thread from every twig.

'That's my life,' said Jack, 'since I first went to sea. I measure it in fish, in case I ever lose count. There'll be another one soon.' He pointed at a low table, where a bone-handled knife lay beside a piece of driftwood.

I looked at what else lay on the table: a brass compass, a folding telescope and a small wooden ship. Her prow had been carved into a goose's head and neck and the *Flying Goose* was painted in neat letters on her bows.

'It's this ship!' I exclaimed. 'Has it really been to sea?'

'Of course she has.' Jack sounded annoyed. 'What did you think? She may be the *Recumbent Goose* now but she was the *Flying Goose* in her day, terror of the King's Navy.'

'Which king?' I asked.

'Oh, they came and went,' said Jack vaguely.

The little ship's rigging was made out of twigs – the sort of thing you don't want to touch in case it breaks. At the top of the mast, a flag flew: the same flag as I had seen fluttering above me up on deck.

'If that's the skull and crossbones,' I said, 'why is there

only one bone?'

Jack had dropped into a wooden seat, hat tipped over his nose and boots up on the table. He shrugged. 'Appropriate, don't you think? One cross Bone . . .'

I frowned. 'How d'you know my name?'

'Who says I was talking about you? But I do know your name – I'd bet my ship on it.' Jack's one eye watched me from under his hat. 'Your name is Dandelion Bone.'

'Yes,' I admitted. 'But most people call me Dan. Except for my sister when she's being annoying – and Aunt Grusilla.'

'*Grusilla! Gru-si-i-i-lla!*'

We both jumped. The parrot had settled in the tree, helping itself to popcorn from a silver goblet wedged between the branches. Now it spread its wings, shrieking, making the leaves shiver and the little fish dance.

'Son of a sea biscuit! I wish he wouldn't do that,' complained Jack. 'The Beak is an excellent mimic. He sounds exactly like m— your uncle.'

I looked at him in surprise. 'Uncle Dandelion? Do you know him, then?'

'You could say so.' Jack tipped his hat lower over his nose. 'Not that I have set foot in the Hall for a very long time . . . The Beak must have escaped from there. He arrived through that porthole one day in a terrible state. The crows were mobbing him. He wouldn't say anything except *Pretty Polly* and *Onion Stuffing*.'

'*Sunday roast*,' said the parrot tragically. '*Pâte on toast*.'

'How long have you been at the Hall?' Jack was looking at my hands. Was I imagining it, or was he counting my fingers?

'Only since yesterday.' It seemed a lot longer. 'We didn't ask to come. Nobody gave us any choice. Mum and Dad . . . had an accident.'

'That was convenient,' murmured Jack.

'There's nothing *convenient*,' I said stiffly, 'about your parents being eaten by cannibals.'

'Depends on the parents,' said Jack. 'But I didn't mean to be rude. I meant it was convenient for your aunt. The Hall must have an Heir – suppose something were to happen to your uncle? *Here lives and breathes a true-born Bone, Or these walls crumble, stone by stone* . . . and all that.'

'Dad was Dandelion Bone too,' I pointed out. 'He could have been the Heir.'

'That wouldn't have suited your aunt at all,' said Jack. 'She wouldn't want a grown man coming to live at the Hall – too old to be kept in his place and told what to do. But you're perfect. And, with no parents, you're in her power for ever.'

'Not for ever! Only until I grow up.' No way was I living with Aunt Grusilla five minutes longer than I needed to.

'Unless you grow up,' agreed Jack.

'It's not as if Aunt Grusilla even *likes* children,' I went on. 'She makes the Grub sleep in the attic.' My hand flew to my mouth. *The Grub!* I'd been gone for ages. It must be awake by now, crying and crying in its cot, and nobody there to hear it. 'I have to get back!'

I'd already turned for the door, but Jack was on his feet in a flash. I stared at his hand on my arm: the black velvet glove with its empty hole.

'Not so fast, Mr Bone. I can't just let you go.'

'But the Grub!' I was desperate. 'It's only a baby, and it's all on its own! I promised I'd look after it. If Aunt Grusilla and Pokiss hear it crying . . . you don't know what they're like!'

'I do,' said Jack grimly. 'But I can't let you go back to the Hall. Nobody needs to know I'm here. You'll talk.'

'I won't. I won't breathe a word, I promise. Bones keep their promises.'

'Huh!' said Jack. 'I can't risk it. I don't know whose side you're on.'

I didn't want to be on anybody's side: just mine and Martha's and the Grub's. 'I'm not on *their* side,' I said, 'if you mean Aunt Grusilla and Pokiss.' I was sure about that. 'But why should I be on yours? You hung me upside down in a net. That's all I know about you.'

'Is it?' Jack looked at me with his one eye, twirling the end of his moustache. 'We'll play a game,' he decided. 'I'll let you go – if you can guess my name.'

'Black Jack?' I said hopefully.

'That's what they called me on the High Seas – when sailors shook in their shoes at the sight of my flag. But I had another name once. Can't you guess? I'll give you a clue. Look at me, Dandelion Bone.'

I wasn't sure I wanted to. His eyepatch was dangling from his fingers.

'Look into my eyes,' he ordered. 'Both of them.'

I swallowed, took a deep breath, and looked.

Glinting in Jack's right eye socket was something smooth and silvery. I could see my reflection in it, the way you can in the back of a spoon.

'Keep looking,' ordered Jack.

I don't spend a lot of time staring into mirrors; it's really not that interesting. I have two eyes, a nose and mouth, in that order, with an ear on each side. Same as most people. My hair's the colour of darkling beetles (says Mum). My eyes are green like shield bugs (says Dad).

I switched my attention to Jack. Close up, he looked

younger – much younger. And there it was again: that feeling that I knew him from somewhere.

'*Oh* . . .' I looked at my own reflection, then back at Jack. If you took away the moustache, and the silver eyeball . . . it was the Family Resemblance. 'I *knew* I'd seen you before. I didn't know where. You're a Bone.' I stared at him. 'I bet your name's Dandelion too. And you're older than me. That makes *you* the Heir. Not me.'

'No.' Jack let go of my shoulders and shook his head. 'I'm a Bone – you're right about that, so you win the game. But my name's not Dandelion and I'm not the Heir. I can't be.'

'Why not?'

'Because,' said Jack, and took off his hat. Darkling beetle hair, the same as mine – except that he had loads of it, falling all the way down his back.

It took me a minute, to see what I was looking at. 'But—' I said, then stopped. I didn't want to be rude. It's better not to mention it, when ladies have moustaches.

'Oh, that.' Jack stroked it. 'If your moustache is fierce enough, people leave you alone. If you're a runaway, alone in the world, that can be useful. My very first moustache I made myself, out of rat. It was a scruffy thing – the rat had died of old age, I think; it had gone rather bald. *This* one was made for me by the wife of a

Peruvian llama farmer.'

'You ran away? Where from?' But I'd already guessed the answer. 'I *do* know who you are: you're Jacobina Bone. Aunt Grusilla's daughter. The one who was never heard of again.'

'Not by that name,' agreed Jack. 'I've had several others, over the years.'

I frowned. 'I don't see why you can't be the Heir, just because you're a girl.'

'Tradition,' said Jack. 'Daundelyon Hall has been passed down, father to son, ever since Sir Lyon's day. I was an only child. My mother didn't want a daughter; she hated me for not being born a boy.'

'So you ran away.' I didn't blame her. 'What made you come back?'

'There is something I need, at Daundelyon Hall,' said Jack carefully. 'It's mine. They took it, without asking. I want it back. It's important. You could say . . . a matter of life and death.'

'What is it?' I asked. 'I can look for it, if you tell me what it is.'

'That's the trouble.' Sighing, Jack helped herself to the parrot's popcorn. 'I don't know. I know what it *was*, when they took it, and I know what it *does*. I'm not sure what it may have turned into, after all these years.'

I didn't think she could have been gone from the

Hall that long. She looked much younger than I had first thought: not more than about fifteen. 'How old were you when you ran away?'

'Age doesn't mean much,' said Jack. 'Not at Daundelyon Hall.'

She led the way back up on deck. The wood was full of the patter of raindrops landing on leaves. I thought of Martha, out there tied to a tree, wet and cold.

'Them and their stupid unicorns!' I said crossly. 'I don't believe Lady Clotilda ever caught one; I reckon she made the whole thing up. They can't honestly think there's one out here, just because of a thousand-year-old story and some hoof prints . . .'

'I can explain the hoof prints,' said Jack. Leaning over the ship's rail, she pointed at something below us. A white beast with long hairy ears and a tufted tail was lipping at a blackberry bush. 'I call him Barnacle,' she said, 'because he lives under my ship. He'll have had another name once. He was a working donkey, giving rides on the beach. He didn't like it much, so he left. We're all runaways here: me, the Beak and the Barnacle.'

Jack took me back along her zip wire, with the Beak flying ahead of us. I had just wobbled to a stop in the boughs of a tall beech tree when I saw a patch of red below me, not far away: the hood of a red raincoat.

I knew that raincoat. It was Martha.

CHAPTER
SEVEN

Martha was sitting on the ground, tied to the trunk of a chestnut tree. She hadn't seen me. Head bent, she was arranging a little pile of conkers. Hanging on to a branch, I leant out from my tree and was about to call her name when Jack stopped me, her hand over my mouth.

'Murrr-*hur*!' I mumbled against her black velvet palm, trying to shake her off.

'Sssh.' I could feel the llama fur moustache tickling my ear. 'Look!'

A black umbrella was weaving through the trees. Pokiss. Reaching Martha, she stood with hands on hips, elbows all angles.

'*One, two, three, four, five; catch a unicorn alive. Six, seven, eight, nine, ten; then you let it go again.* Well?' demanded Pokiss. 'Did it come?'

'What do you think?' Martha was cross.

'Wrong sort of maiden,' sniffed Pokiss. 'Not virtuous enough.'

'Actually,' said Martha, 'a whole *herd* of unicorns came. The biggest one is hiding behind that tree. I didn't catch him because he is my friend. If you come any closer, he'll stab you with his horn.'

Pokiss wasn't fooled. She shrugged, turning back the way she had come. 'Sssuit yourself. Sssee you tomorrow. Unless the wolves see you first . . .'

Martha lasted for several seconds, then gave in. 'Wait!' she called to the departing umbrella. 'Take me with you! Please?'

'Hoity toity, make your mind up,' mocked Pokiss, but she turned back and began unknotting the rope. When Martha was free, with just a loop around her middle, Pokiss took hold of the loose end and jerked it. 'Walkies!'

'I'm not a *dog*,' complained Martha, but she stood up and followed Pokiss through the bracken.

'She'll expect me to be at the Hall, waiting for her,' I warned Jack. 'If she makes a fuss, they'll all start wondering where I am. I wasn't supposed to cross the drawbridge; Aunt Grusilla is going to be angry.'

'She won't know,' said Jack. 'I'll take you back another way. There's a tunnel – it comes out in the middle of the maze.'

'That's how you got in this morning?' I guessed. 'Did you come to look for your lost whatever-it-is?'

'It didn't help much,' sighed Jack. 'I don't have a clue where to start.'

We came out of the woods, on to the edge of the river. Across the water, the old castle walls rose up from the bank. We were facing the back of the Hall, out of sight of the gatehouse or any of the windows. Jack parted a clump of bracken and heaved on a rope, pulling out a small round rowing boat with *Ship's Biscuit* painted on the side.

Fat raindrops spotted the surface of the river with ripples as Jack paddled us across. On the other side, she looped the *Biscuit's* rope around the trunk of a twisted lilac, so we could scramble out. Halfway up the steep bank, Jack parted a curtain of ivy and brambles, revealing a black hole – like the entrance to a giant rabbit burrow.

We had to stoop: Jack first, with me at her heels. She picked up a lantern; a match flared and light flickered over the low ceiling and damp, musty walls, setting strange shadows dancing.

'*Cannelloni pepperoni!*' said the parrot darkly, fluffing up its feathers against the rain. '*Nada enchilada!*' And it flapped away to the branches of the lilac tree.

I don't know how long it took us to wend our way through that tunnel: long enough to make me want fresh air and the chance to stand up straight. Then the darkness and fustiness began to fade and we were at the foot of some steps, a pale square of daylight opening out above us. The steps brought us out into a circle of white stone pillars, at the back of a plinth with a stone lady standing on it. She had hardly any clothes on and was holding a bunch of grapes.

'Venus, goddess of love,' said Jack. 'My father had this temple built. And guess who the model was for the statue?'

I peered up at the marble face and curvy shoulders. I didn't want to stare at anything lower down. 'Oh, it's Aunt Grusilla . . . !'

'A long time ago,' said Jack. 'Longer than you'd think. Come on.' She pointed to where the tall hedges of the maze rose up outside the little temple. 'I'll show you the way out.'

She strode ahead of me, through the maze's twists and U-turns, without making any mistakes.

'The exit's that way,' she said, as we rounded a final corner. 'Goodbye, Dandelion Bone.'

'Wait,' I said. 'We'll see each other again, won't we? We're cousins . . . sort of. Family.'

'Family . . .' Jack repeated. 'I never had much of a family.' She hesitated, twisting the llama fur moustache, then seemed to make up her mind. 'Maybe you should know. Maybe it's only fair to tell you . . .'

'Tell me what?'

'The day after tomorrow: it's All Hallows' Eve . . .'

'Halloween,' I agreed. 'I knew *that*!'

'Things happen at Daundelyon Hall,' Jack was choosing her words carefully. 'At Halloween.'

It was raining harder now. I felt the wind brush cold against my skin.

'You mean bad things?' I asked.'

'Yes . . . or no. It depends on how you look at it.' Jack's one eye didn't meet mine. She was looking down at her hands, spreading her nine fingers.

'The *fingers*!' I said. 'You've all got one missing, the whole lot of you. *What happens to them?*'

'That,' said Jack, 'is what I mean to discover.'

'That's what you're looking for?' I stared at her. 'That's what you came back for? Your *finger*? But how did you lose it?'

'You'll find out,' said Jack. 'Soon enough.'

'*Dandelion? Dandelion Bone!*' It was Aunt Grusilla. I could hear Lambkin yapping. 'Are you out here? Where are you?'

'They're looking for you.' Jack was already melting backwards into the maze.

'You have to tell me what you mean.' I caught hold of her sleeve. 'You can't say stuff like that and then just *leave*!'

'All right, but not now.' Jack relented. 'Meet me tomorrow. Three o'clock, in the Temple of Venus. I'll mark your way through the maze.' Digging in her pocket, she brought out a handful of shiny yellow coins. 'Just follow the trail.'

I blinked at the coins. 'Are those chocolate?'

'Only gold. Sorry.'

'*Dandelion?*'

Lambkin's barks were getting closer. I turned my head to listen. When I turned back again, Jack was gone.

'*There* you are at last, Dandelion!' Aunt Grusilla came billowing up, holding a pink tasselled umbrella carefully over her hair.

'I was in the maze,' I said, trying to look innocent. 'It's easy to get lost in there, isn't it?'

Which wasn't – quite – a lie.

I could hear the Grub roaring from halfway up the

attic stairs. Martha was with him, frowning ferociously in a long apron and a white cap.

'I thought you'd *gone*,' she said furiously. 'Like Caramel. I thought you'd run away on your own, without us.'

'I wouldn't. Why are you dressed like that?'

'Aunt Grusilla says the unicorns don't like me because I'm not *good* enough. She says doing lots of housework will make me good-er,' growled Martha. 'They made me scrub the kitchen floor. Poke-Hiss watched me the *whole* time, so I couldn't even look in the fridge for something to eat. It was *ages* before she let me go. I looked for you, but you weren't anywhere, so I came up here in case there were any more bananas. The Grub was crying, so I stayed. Anyway, my leg was hurting.'

I remembered Pokiss driving the silver pin into the little wax doll and felt a flutter, like cold breath, on the back of my neck. 'What's the matter with your leg?'

'Don't know. It just hurts.'

Glancing out of the window, I saw a figure dressed in black, hunched up against the rain, hobbling towards the Glass House. 'The funeral must be over. Boy's back.'

His top hat was pulled down over his ears and there was a cat at his heels: the grey one I'd seen in the stables.

I remembered what else I had seen in the stables.

'Martha, I found Caramel's bike! They'd tried to hide it under a load of hay. Caramel's still here, somewhere; she has to be.'

'They're keeping her prisoner,' said Martha fiercely. 'We have to rescue her!'

'We have to find her first,' I pointed out.

Martha had joined me by the window, watching Boy and the cat.

'Where's he going?'

I shrugged. 'That Glass House, probably. He's the gardener, isn't he? *Ow*!'

Martha was gripping my arm. 'Meatballs! Don't you see? That's where Caramel is – she must be! They've hidden her in the Glass House!'

The cat was winding around Boy's legs, wanting to be let in. 'Aunt Grusilla did say not to go in there . . .' I said, watching Boy shoo it away.

'To stop us from finding her!' Martha was triumphant. 'Why else would she care?'

'It's made of *glass*,' I reminded her. 'Who hides anything – anybody – in a building you can see through? Anyway, Caramel would be able to smash her way out . . .'

'Not if they've tied her up.' Martha was fizzing with excitement. 'Come on, quick, we have to rescue her before it gets too dark!'

'We can't, not while Boy's in there,' I objected.

'We'll have to distract him,' said Martha. 'I can tell him my jokes. While he's busy laughing, you rescue Caramel.'

'That might work,' I agreed, 'if you knew more than about six jokes. And if any of them were actually funny.'

'They *are* funny,' argued Martha. 'What stinks and rhymes with *boo*? You!'

Her jokes were all a bit like that. 'It's not me that stinks; it's the Grub again,' I told her. 'We can't go anywhere until we've changed it.'

'Stop making excuses.' She was already on her way out of the door. 'You're just scared of getting into trouble with Aunt Gruesome. Cowardy Chicken, Dan-Dandy-Dandelion!'

She knows I hate that. *Dent de Lyon*: Tooth of the Lion, I reminded myself. Razor-sharp and dangerous, that was me. Yeah, right.

The Grub really did stink. I had to breathe through my mouth, so the smell didn't get stuck in my nose. I sighed. Sir Lyon de Beaune might have got top marks for sword-slashing, mace-bashing and chopping people up but I was ready to bet he'd never had to change a nappy.

I finished de-squelching the Grub and zipped it into its yellow duck rain suit. Through the window, I could see Martha running towards the Glass House, Mum's cardigan flapping out behind her. Creeping down the stairs, I crossed my fingers that Aunt Grusilla was still busy with her giant knickers while Pokiss nailed coffins together or fried bats' wings for our supper. The oak doors creaked and groaned as I pushed them open, just wide enough to let me through. The rain hurled itself at me, stinging my face. I pulled up the Grub's hood, then my own, and slipped out.

Martha was dripping wet, with her hair hanging in mousetails and her nose pressed against the Glass House wall.

'I can't see properly,' she complained, rubbing at the streaking raindrops and squashing her nose even flatter. 'There's loads of stuff growing in there – it's like the rainforest. Where's Boy?'

Behind the glass was a green-lit world full of leaves and vines and tangling tendrils. Exotic creeper-y things swarmed up pillars and dangled long tentacles from the high glass ceiling.

KEEP OUT, said the sign on the door. Martha's hand was already on the handle.

'Wait,' I said. 'Let's have a look around the outside first.'

We edged around the glass walls, peering in through the jungle of plants.

'There's Boy!' said Martha at last. 'What's he sitting on?'

I rubbed at the glass. Boy was perched on top of a high, flat-topped block of stone. I looked at the faded letters cut into its side, the ivy trailing over it, and I knew exactly what it was. I knew what the pale shapes wedged into the ground around it were too. If you grow up with parents whose idea of fun is an afternoon spent hunting for the Rufous Grasshopper and the White-letter Hairstreak Butterfly, you get to spend a lot of time hanging around in cemeteries.

'It's a tomb.' I said.

'But,' said Martha, 'who puts dead people in a greenhouse?'

'Or – who builds a glass house on top of a graveyard? Those are old graves. See the stones: they're all crooked and mossy. Hey, what's he doing?'

Boy had his upturned hat beside him on top of the tomb. Reaching inside it, he pulled out a string of sausages. Picking up a pair of garden snippers, he snipped a sausage off the end and with a flick of the wrist sent it spinning into the creeping green thicket. There was a rippling of leaves.

Another sausage. Another flick of the wrist. Another ripple.

'What is it?' whispered Martha. 'What's in there?'

'Whatever it is,' I said, 'I don't think it's Caramel.'

'I'm going to ask him what he's doing!' Martha was turning back for the door when we heard something that made us both stiffen.

'Boy? Garden Boy? Are you in there?' It was Aunt Grusilla, shaking raindrops off her umbrella.

Boy jolted upright as if he'd been electrified. Tossing the sausages into his hat, he rammed it back on to his head and slid off the tomb. Snatching up a garden spade, he began frantically shovelling a mound of earth into a long, rectangular hole.

Aunt Grusilla pushed her way through the palm trees, Lambkin squashed under one arm, and peered down into the hole.

'*Where* is Bessie Fleaspoon?' she demanded. 'Why isn't she down there?'

Boy hung his head. 'She be in her coffin, m'lady. In the graveyard at Witches' Cross – in the corner, where the daffodils first bloom in the spring.'

'You old fool!' Aunt Grusilla's chins wobbled with rage. 'Dunderhead! You know how it works. You take the body *out* of the coffin. You fill the coffin with potatoes, so it's heavy. You drive the *potatoes* to the funeral; the body's buried here, to nourish the earth, and what people don't know they can't complain about. How difficult is that to remember? You've been doing it long enough. What is the point of digging a grave and filling it in again, if there's no *body* in it?'

"Twere Bessie's funeral,' quavered Boy, twisting his bony hands together. "'Tain't fair if a person can't be buried at their own funeral. It's wrong, what we do, my lady. A body has its rights, even when the soul has flown. Disrespectful. That's what it is.'

'Humdudgeon!' snapped Aunt Grusilla, dumping the wriggling Lambkin and very nearly tipping him into the grave. 'This is where the Bones of Daundelyon Hall are buried. It's an honour for Bessie Fleaspoon and her sort to be allowed to join them. How can it be wrong? It's Nature. Ashes to ashes, dust to dust. Compost to compost. The Circle of Life. The plants growing in here need rich soil. Flesh, blood and bone. They can't flourish, if they're not fed. You're the gardener – you should know that. It's your job to look after them.'

'I do look after 'em,' whined Boy. 'I tuck 'em into their flower beds at night, as if they were my own flesh and blood, my own little chickies. I water 'em and whisper tender things to 'em. There's never a day, my lady, when those Cabbages go hungry.'

There was a burst of excited yapping from Lambkin, who had disappeared into the ferns. He emerged, tail wagging, with a sausage in his mouth.

Boy snatched it away from him, holding it behind his back.

'Give that to me *now*,' demanded Aunt Grusilla, holding out her hand. 'Or I shall call Pokiss and she will give you such an attack of pinch-cramps and pox-pustules, you won't sleep for a month.'

Cowering, Boy handed over his sausage. Aunt Grusilla held it between finger and thumb, the feathers in her hair bobbing angrily. She turned on Boy, who hopped behind a potted palm for safety.

'Nincompoop!' she told him fiercely. 'What do you think you are doing? The Halloweeds need blood and bone – not sausages! Especially now, with those weevils eating their leaves and chewing at their roots. You noodle-headed buffoon! Is it any wonder that they're wilting?' She hurled the sausage into the empty grave. Lambkin danced along the edge, yapping and drooling.

'There's no harm in it, m'lady.' Boy peered out from between the spiky palm leaves. 'I do a spot of weeding for Missus Horsefeather, the butcher's wife, now and then – she pays me in sausages. The Cabbages gobble them up. I've done as you told me for a good many years, m'lady, but I'll not do it for the likes of Bessie Fleaspoon: not when I've known her all her life, since she were a twig of a girl, with always a kind word and a smile for me. I'll not sneak the dead in here any more, m'lady, leaving their loved ones a-sorrowin' by an empty grave. 'Tisn't right. It annoys the angels. When a soul's lived as long as I, he doesn't want to be on the wrong side of no angels.'

Aunt Grusilla folded her arms across her front, her face as stormy as the sky. 'I am disappointed in you, Boy. Sir Dandelion always said you had green fingers.'

'Ten of 'em, once upon a time,' muttered Boy.

'You know how important it is that these plants are kept alive,' said Aunt Grusilla coldly. 'Must I remind you that we have had one Unfortunate Accident already?'

'That weren't my fault! 'Twere the steak pudding what did it, m'lady,' pleaded Boy. 'You know I'd never hurt one of the Cabbages a-purpose. Missus Horsefeather gave me a pudding all o' my own, after I trimmed her hedges. I were sittin' eatin' it. Only turned my back for a moment, to put the cat out. She follows me in here, sometimes, for the warmth. How were I to know Cabbages like steak pudding? And a naughty, greedy Cabbage to go swallowing it whole like that! Tried my best to save it, m'lady – pudding too – but there was naught to be done. It choked to death.'

'And look what happened to Sir Dandelion because of it!' said Aunt Grusilla sternly. 'We have paid you well for your work here . . .'

'Threepence a week,' mumbled Boy, staring at his feet.

'We have paid you in Time. Isn't that more precious than threepences?'

Boy clasped his nine remaining fingers together. 'Time's a pretty thing when you're young and nimble. It's not so shiny-bright when your joints creak and your bones ache and your hair's blowing away in the wind like thistle seeds and you've spat out most of your teeth. 'Tis flying in the face of Nature to make a person go on and on, when his only wish is to lie down quietly, snuff out the candle and let his old bones rest in peace. I hear feathers rustling in the night – 'tis the angels, come to take me, but you won't let me go. We're meant to take our turn and move on, not hang about where we don't belong, like frost in May. Even you, my lady . . .'

He'd gone too far. Aunt Grusilla snatched up the garden spade, waving it like a weapon. 'I'll dig you up,' she threatened. 'I'll chop you down!'

'Not my Cabbage – don't harm it, m'lady!' Boy clasped his hands together, pleading. 'It's never done no wrong, other than what's in its nature. Do what you like to me – I've waited long enough – but let the Cabbages be!'

Who knows what would have happened next, if the Grub hadn't got bored in my arms and let out a squawk.

As Boy and Aunt Grusilla turned their heads, we ducked out of sight.

'Quick!' I whispered to Martha. 'Back to the house. Run!'

CHAPTER EIGHT

We got back to the house, soaked and breathless, to find Pokiss at the foot of the stairs, polishing a suit of armour with a feather duster. The feathers were blue and gold and looked a lot like parrot.

'Sssupper,' she said. 'Last to sit down gets ssseconds,' she threatened, prodding at us with her duster.

Aunt Grusilla was the last to sit down at the table. She didn't seem to notice that we were dripping wet. You could tell she was in a bad mood. In between mouthfuls she pressed her lips together in a thin, angry line, her fur eyebrows and spider-leg eyelashes bristling spitefully. Pokiss sniffed, hissing under her breath as she dolloped food on to our plates. It was hard to tell what it was but I thought I was safe with the bits of mushroom – until one of them put out feelers and turned into a slug.

The meal seemed to go on for a very long time; nobody spoke. I was trying to make sense, in my head, of what we had seen and heard in the Glass House. Aunt Grusilla and Pokiss had been using their fake Funeral business to get hold of bodies. I forked my slugs about, feeling a bit sick. They buried the bodies in the Glass House – but *why*? And what – or *who* – were the sausages for? I peered around the dead lilies: Martha was twisting a tangle of what looked like pondweed around her fork, her nose wrinkled up as far as it would go.

When Aunt Grusilla had finished eating, she scraped back her chair and stamped away without saying goodnight. Pokiss sniffed as she cleared our full plates, but didn't say anything. The Grub was rubbing its eyes.

'We can't leave it in the attic all by itself,' I said as we tramped up the stairs. 'It can sleep in my room.'

Martha was shivering; Mum's cardigan had stopped smelling of Mum and started to smell of wet dog.

'You'll have to take it off,' I told her. 'You can't wear it for the rest of your life.'

'Can if I want,' said Martha, and shut herself in her

room without offering to help with the Grub.

When I'd finished nappy-wrestling and push-pulled the Grub into its sleepsuit, I tucked it up in one of my drawers and pulled the string on the musical mouse. As soon as I saw its eyes close, *Twinkle, Twinkle, Little Star* still playing, I went to see Martha. She was sitting up in bed, her dinosaurs around her, drawing.

'It's Mum and Dad and the cannibals,' she explained, when she saw me looking. 'All eating peanut butter sandwiches. They're vegetarian cannibals.'

'You can't have vegetarian cannibals,' I objected.

'It's my picture,' said Martha. 'I can have what I like. Dan, what was Aunt Grusilla telling Boy off for, in the Glass House? What had he done? And who was eating the sausages?'

I looked at her: she was biting her thumbnail, dark smudges of tiredness under her eyes. I heard Mum's voice in my head: *look after Martha, won't you, Dan . . . ?*

'There's a cat,' I said. 'I expect it was the cat.'

It wasn't. You know it wasn't. Boy shut the cat out. I didn't want to think about it. Not now, with the darkness pressing in around us and twigs scratching like claws on the walls. I could hear the *tck tck tck* of the Deathwatch Beetle.

A death in the house . . .

An empty grave in the Glass House.

And we still hadn't found Caramel.

'I don't think Caramel's in the Glass House,' I told her. 'But she can't be far away. We'll find her tomorrow.'

'I want her *now*.' Martha frowned at her dinosaurs. 'She tells me stories at bedtime.'

I sighed. 'All right, I'll tell you a story.'

'Go on, then,' said Martha.

I picked up a plastic diplodocus. My mind had gone blank. 'Er – OK, once upon a time . . .'

'I'm not *five*!' A stegosaurus and a parasaurolophus toppled off the bed as Martha yanked the bedclothes up around her chin. 'Caramel tells me *proper* stories. Ghost stories. Horror stories. Uncle Roly's teeth.'

'Not Uncle Roly,' I said firmly. Martha had nagged at Caramel until she'd finally given in and told us the terrible tale of Uncle Roly. I'd had a nightmares afterwards, about being eaten alive by sets of feral false teeth.

In the end I told her what had happened that afternoon in the Deepness: about a pirate ship in the treetops and a girl called Jacobina Bone, who had run away to sea and become Black Jack.

'You're rubbish at stories,' said Martha sleepily, when I'd finished. 'You said it was *true*.'

'It *is* true. I'm meeting her in the maze tomorrow afternoon. You can see for yourself.'

Martha had burrowed down under her bedclothes. The wind was blowing in through the open window, lifting the curtains away from the sill – which is why I noticed the pale blob in the corner of the sill: Pokiss's little wax doll, with the pin still sticking in its leg.

'What are you doing?' asked Martha.

'Nothing.' I leant out of the window, pulling the pin free and letting it drop into the darkness. 'Does your leg still hurt?'

Dinosaurs scattered as Martha gave an experimental kick. 'It was hurting when I got into bed. It's all right now.'

I dug in my pocket for the blue bead, the last of Caramel's charms against Evil. It wasn't there. *It must have fallen out while I was hanging upside down in the Deepness. The only thing we had to keep us safe from Pokiss. Unless . . .*

'Martha, I need your blue pen,' I said urgently.

She looked at me in surprise. 'There. On the floor. I drew Mum wearing her cardigan . . . Ouch – what are you doing?'

'Keep still.' Snatching at the pen, I yanked the bedclothes back, grabbing her arm and rolling up her sleeve. 'I'm giving you a lucky Eye. Like Caramel's.'

'What for?' demanded Martha, pulling away. 'Only if you tell me why.'

'*This* is why,' I told her, and held up the wax doll. I didn't want to scare her, but I could tell she was going to be difficult if I didn't. 'It's supposed to be you. Pokiss made it. Then she stuck a pin in it – just *there*.' I pointed at the doll's left leg. I wanted to squash the whole thing back into a ball, but I was a bit worried about what that might do to Martha. '*Now* will you let me draw an Eye on you? It'll keep bad wishes away – Caramel said so.'

Martha didn't argue after that. She sat quietly, staring at the doll and rubbing her own left knee until I'd finished, then took the pen from me. The blue Eye she gave me, sketched just above my elbow, looked more like Caramel's than the one I'd drawn on her. She's better at art than I am.

'Dan,' she said, as I was heading back to my own room.

'What?'

'That thing Poke-Hiss did with the doll, hurting me – I'll make her sorry. I'll get my own back. You wait and see.'

The Grub woke and cried in the night. Rain was rattling the window frame, beating against the diamond panes. Padding barefoot across the splintery floorboards, I drew the curtains back and looked out towards the Deepness. I wondered if Jack and her parrot were sleeping, aboard the *Recumbent Goose*. Moonlight broke through a tear in the clouds and flickered on the swirling river. Shivering, I closed the curtains and jumped back into bed, taking the Grub with me.

It felt like no time at all before I woke again, with a start. The Grub was snoring peacefully, bunched up in my bedclothes, but there were loud noises coming from Martha's room, next door.

'Meatballs! I won't!' The day hadn't even started and Martha was already in a Fuss. 'Why should I?'

Something thudded, hard, against the wall. It was followed by another crash, then another, and a familiar *Tssss!*

'Nasssty!' hissed Pokiss.

Wide awake now, I rolled out of bed. Next door, Martha was throwing dinosaurs. I ducked as a velociraptor sailed out into the corridor, grazing my ear. Pokiss was holding the apron and cap Martha had been made to wear the day before, and a plastic tyrannosaurus rex. When they saw me, they both started complaining at once.

'Throwing things at poor Pokiss!' Pokiss pointed the tyrannosaurus accusingly at Martha. There was a red mark on her cheek. 'Not nicesss!'

'She wants me to do her stupid scrubbing,' grumbled Martha. 'I don't want to. I haven't finished being asleep.'

Pokiss peeled back the blankets, grabbed Martha by the ear and tugged.

'Owww!' wailed Martha. She reached for a dinosaur, but she'd used up all the sharp ones.

'Ssslug-a-bed,' said Pokiss. 'Downstairs before the porridge boils. Pygmy best do as she's told. Auntsy in a temper. Not nicesss.' Dropping cap and apron at Martha's feet, she stalked past me and down the corridor, fluffy slippers flip-flapping on the floorboards.

Martha, left standing there in her pyjamas, looked like a thundercloud. She took a deep breath and opened her mouth.

'Don't,' I begged, before she could start yelling. 'Aunt Grusilla's already talking about sending you to the North Pole, to a Home for Unsatisfactory Children.'

'I don't care if she does!' said Martha. 'I'll run away and be raised by polar bears. It would be better than being here!'

'No, it wouldn't,' I said firmly. 'You'd freeze. You haven't got the right sort of fur. And polar bears don't eat pizza. You'd have to eat raw seal: it's in the food chain. Please, Martha – I need you to help me look for Caramel. Do what they want and get it over with, then we can start looking for clues.'

To my relief, Martha let her breath go. 'Why do I have to be their slave, and not you?' she complained? 'Just because you're the stupid Heir!' She puffed out her cheeks in an impression of Aunt Grusilla. 'Preshus Weshus little Dandelion, come and be tickled by my Hairy-Fairy chin whiskers and smell my dead-mouse breath!'

Pokiss was waiting at the top of the stairs, holding a long, twiggy broom. 'Sssweep sweep!' she ordered, pointing down the corridor.

Martha scowled under her cap, but didn't argue.

I went back to my room, where the Grub was awake, chewing its toes and gurgling at Robo-Ancestor. I had just got to the end of another nappy-fight when the door burst open. Aunt Grusilla was standing in the doorway.

'I have come for the *Dent de Lyon*,' she announced. 'It has a job to do.'

As she prised Sir Lyon's sword out of his metal hand, I couldn't help staring at her hair. Today it was piled up around a silver clock, its hands frozen at five past one, and topped with a spray of blue and gold feathers.

'Aunt, are those *parrot* feathers?'

'You are admiring my *coiffure*?' Aunt Grusilla patted her hair, looking pleased. 'Pokiss arranges it for me.

Your Uncle Dandelion used to own a pair of parrots. Terrible birds. The hen laid an egg in my hair one day – that was the end of Pretty Polly. I wrung her neck and told Pokiss to cook her. Stuffed with onions. The other one escaped, or I'd have done the same to him.' The feathers swayed and nodded as she swiped the air with the Lion's Tooth.

'What do you need the sword for?' I asked.

'A spot of gardening,' said Aunt Grusilla. 'In the Glass House.'

I went down to breakfast, my head aching with too many questions. Where was Caramel? What was it that lived in the Glass House and ate sausages? Who uses a sword to do the gardening? What happened to all those missing fingers – and what was it that Jack had been trying to warn me about . . . ?

Lambkin was lying nose-on-paws by the bottom step, whining.

'What's up, Lambkin?' As I bent to pat him, he rolled his eyes at me and growled.

'He doesn't like being called Lambkin,' said Martha, from the top of the stairs. She was standing astride her broom, as if she were hoping it might take off. 'It's embarrassing for him. He'd rather have a fiercer name. Like Wolfsnarl.' Dismounting from her broomstick, she came downstairs. 'Hey, Wolfsnarl!' Crouching down in front of him, she held out her hand. The feathery tail stirred.

'Martha, look at his tail!' I hadn't noticed before, but something wasn't right. 'He's like the rest of them: he's got a bit missing!' I parted the long hair, feeling for the tip – which wasn't there. Lambkin-Wolfsnarl gave another growl.

'You're annoying him,' said Martha. 'How would you like having your tail tweaked? Listen, Dan, I *found* something! When I was sweeping.'

'Riding your broomstick, you mean.'

'I had to *pretend* to do some sweeping,' said Martha, 'because Pokiss was watching. But then she went through this door and I saw . . .'

'Tssss!' Pokiss was standing behind us. 'Ssscrubbery,' she ordered, grasping Martha's collar. 'Potsies and pansies don't wash themselvsies.'

It was just me and the Grub, in its highchair, sitting at the long table for breakfast.

The Grub seemed to quite like the porridge, but I didn't think Mum would have approved of it swallowing the 'raisins'. I was brushing the gunk off their wings and letting them fly away when I heard Aunt Grusilla's voice.

'Pokiss! *Pokiss!* Come and pull my boots off. They're

covered in mud.'

'Tsss . . . is it done?' I heard Pokiss hiss. 'Sssnicker-snack?'

'Sliced right through,' answered Aunt Grusilla. 'One less set of roots to feed. A gardener must get rid of the dead wood – and if it wasn't dead before, it is now.'

'Halloweeds won't like it,' sniffed Pokiss. 'Old man's cared for them since they were cuttings, no taller than a daisy. He knew their ways; they knew his.'

'Piffle!' declared Aunt Grusilla. 'Boy allowed those plants to run wild. Vegetables are like children: they require discipline and putting in their place. Gardening is very hard work; now my hair is out of place. You must come upstairs, Pokiss, and help me put it right.'

Batting away the cloud of rescued raisins buzzing around my head, I could hear the sound of footsteps on their way up the stairs – which meant that Martha was on her own in the scrubbery. The Grub was happily smearing porridge all over its face and complained when I lifted it out of its highchair.

'Sssh,' I told it. 'We're going to find Martha.'

I went through the door Pokiss used for carrying out plates to and from the kitchen. I hadn't gone far – down some steps and a little way along a cold stone corridor – when I heard a crash.

'Oh, *meatballs*!' said a gloomy voice.

The kitchen was dark and cavernous, with ugly, leering little faces carved into its blackened beams. The fireplace was wide enough to spit-roast an elephant and the iron cooking pot bubbling on the hob was big enough to bath a baby. Whiffs of burnt porridge, slug stew and mice pudding mingled with the smell of sawdust and the tang of wood varnish. Coffins were propped and stacked everywhere. Some of them looked ready to use, shiny-handled with velvet linings; others were still in roughly cut pieces. Leading off the kitchen was a bare little room with nothing in it except a large white enamel sink. Teetering on a pile of books in front of it, with her sleeves rolled up to her elbows, Martha was surrounded by puddles of water and shards of smashed china.

'What are you standing on those books for?'

'Obvious, Stupid.' She flapped her elbows at me; her sleeves were rolled up and her hands covered in soap bubbles up to the wrists. 'I can't reach the taps otherwise.'

'Pygmy.' I had to duck as she threw a greasy spoon at my head.

'Poke-Hiss is making me do *all* the washing-up!' said Martha, outraged. 'And *look* how much there is! I don't think she's done any since we got here – she's been leaving it all for me. I *hate* her!'

I looked at the mess on the floor. 'What did you break?'

'A stupid plate.' Martha pushed back her hair with a soapy hand. 'With the stupid Bone Crest on it. What do you suppose she'll do to me?'

'Nothing,' I said, fetching the broom from the kitchen. 'Because she won't notice.' Plonking the Grub down on the floor, I swept the bits into a coffin and propped the lid back into place. 'There; no one will know. Not until somebody needs burying, anyway. You said you'd found something . . . ?'

Martha dug in her pocket and held out her hand. Resting on her palm was a little scrap of shiny purple paper. 'Chocolate wrapper. It was right at the end of the corridor. Caramel went that way; she must have done. It's a *clue*, Dan.'

'*Tssss . . .*'

Neither of us had noticed the shadow in the doorway. We both jumped, Martha nearly wobbling off her books. She closed her fingers around the scrap of paper, stuffing it back in her pocket, but that wasn't what had caught Pokiss's attention. She was staring at Martha's bare arm, beneath her rolled-up sleeve. And the blue Eye I'd drawn there was staring right back at her.

'Owww!' Martha cried out in pain as Pokiss seized

her elbow and spat on her arm, rubbing at the Eye with the edge of her grubby apron.

'Tssss.' As the ink smeared into a blue smudge, Pokiss hissed so fiercely that the droplet quivering from the end of her nose splashed on to Martha's wrist. 'Tricksssy little pygmies . . .' Dragging Martha into the kitchen, she stuffed her into a white, pink-lined coffin, pushing the kitchen table against it to wedge the lid shut.

I lunged towards it, but Pokiss caught me easily. Pinning me against the sink with one bony knee, she drew on long rubber gloves and pulled up my sleeve, twisting my elbow. Her dishwater eyes narrowed to slits as they found Martha's artwork.

'Nasssty. Massster Dandelion thinks he's oh so clever, thinks he can trick poor Pokiss.' She reached for a scrubbing brush and turned on the tap. 'We'll sssee about that.'

Thrusting my arm into the stream of water, she began to scrub at the Eye above my elbow.

'Ow – you're hurting . . .' The bristles were rough. I struggled, but Pokiss just scrubbed harder.

Shouts and thumps were coming from the white coffin.

'You have to let her out!' I squirmed in Pokiss's grip. 'She can't *breathe* . . .'

'Not supposed to breathe in there. Not what it's for,'

said Pokiss. 'The little mouse will last long enough in her house – if you keep ssstill.'

By the time she let me go, my arm was raw, with beads of blood where the Eye had been. She gave me a shove that sent me sprawling on to the floor beside the Grub, then it was Martha's turn. Bursting out of the coffin, red-faced and panting, she wriggled like an eel. She kicked and clawed and squealed, but there was no escaping Pokiss and her scrubbing brush.

My arm was throbbing and I'd bruised my knees on the stone floor. The Grub was tugging at the cover of one of the books, leaving porridge-y handprints all it. Big and heavy, it was bound in stained leather and looked very old. I glanced at Pokiss. Head bent, soap bubbles flying everywhere, all her attention was on Martha. I pulled the book towards me and opened it up.

The title page was black, with just one word spelt out in carefully inked silver capitals:

GRIMOIRE

The 'G', if you looked at it closely, was a winding snake and the 'I's were bones; the 'M' was an ugly little creature with clawed wings and the 'O' was a skull.

The paper felt like dead leaves between my fingers.

With one eye on Pokiss, I turned the pages, breathing in their dusty-musty smell. The handwriting was sloping and scratchy, the letters all cramped close together, making it difficult to read. I could make out some of the headings:

For Blighting your Neighbour's Turnips

For the Infliction of Warts, Boils and Sundry Painful Swellings upon the Nether Regions

Some of the pages were marked – with what looked like dried rats' tails.

For the Efficacious Use of Unicorn Dung in the Removal of Greater and Lesser Weevils

For the Dismantling of Time . . .

Uneasiness tickled the back of my neck, like spiders' feet. I closed the book, just as Pokiss pushed Martha away and turned to look at the Grub.

'Eyes pie. I ssspy sssomething beginning with *i*! Infant!'

'Why can't you leave us *alone*?' howled Martha. 'You're a horrible old witch. I know what you did yesterday, making my leg hurt, with that little wax person. You think you're so smart and witchy, but just you wait . . . !' Scrabbling in her pocket, she pulled something out. I couldn't think what it was, at first: a small, pale brown blob, a bit squashed, with bits of pocket fluff sticking to it. Then, as she held it up, I realized: Martha had made her own little doll. And I knew who it was supposed to be.

'Sss . . . sss . . . sss . . .' Pokiss was laughing. She went on laughing until Martha picked a fork out of the washing-up pile and jabbed it into her doll's stomach.

I don't know who was most surprised when Pokiss let out a wheezing cry and folded up. Martha looked as startled as anybody.

'Martha, stop!' I said urgently. Pokiss was making terrible gurgling noises, like fighting cats. 'You're murdering her!'

'How was I to know it would *work*?' Martha defended herself. 'Anyway, it serves her right.' But she took the fork out.

Pokiss straightened up again almost immediately, her face pinched and pale. She was staring and staring at Martha.

'*Run!*' I cried, but as we turned for the door, Martha slipped in a puddle of washing-up water. I stopped and put out a hand, yanking her up, but it was too late: I felt Pokiss's cold fingers close around my arm.

As she marched us upstairs, my skin tingled with dread. We'd made her angry; we'd hurt her. What would she do in return . . . ?

She bundled us into Martha's room and confiscated all the colouring pens. Then, after one last long hard stare, she left us alone. I held my breath, sure that she'd at least lock us in, but she didn't.

'Well, that worked well,' sniffed Martha, when we were sure she had really gone and our hearts had stopped racing. 'You and your Eyes. Meatballs. Now I can't even do any colouring.'

'How did you *do* that?' I demanded. 'What did you make that doll out of?'

'Toffee,' admitted Martha. 'Caramel had that box of chocolates and nobody ever wants the toffees. I saved them, just in case. Last night, I was so hungry I thought I might eat them after all but then I had a better idea. I chewed them and chewed them until they went soft. That doll looked just like her, didn't you think? Pointy nose and everything.' She was hopping about, all pleased with herself. 'I'm a *witch*, Dan! A real one!'

'Hmm,' I said. 'It was probably just a coincidence. She'd eaten too many flies, or frogs or mice or something, and had a pain. 'Never mind that now. We have to find Caramel.'

Babies are not helpful on secret missions; we had to wait for the Grub to fall asleep.

'We should probably give it a bath,' I said, looking at its mask of smeared porridge.

'Not *we*,' said Martha. 'You. You're the eldest and I'm

busy. If I were you, I'd just leave it out in the rain for a bit. That'd work.' And she disappeared into her bedroom, shutting the door very firmly behind her.

The bath was old and stained, with a whole family of spiders living in it. I didn't want to drown them, and anyway I couldn't find a plug. In the end, I filled King Charles I's chamber pot with bubble bath and used that. (I rinsed it out first, in case it hadn't been washed since the Royal Wee.) The Grub got bubbles in its eyes. It scrunched up its face and screamed. I didn't know how to make it stop and nobody came to help. By the time I had it dry and dressed again, we were both exhausted. I put it in its drawer, with its musical mouse, and went to find Martha.

She was sitting on her bedroom floor, surrounded by a wobbly circle of white powder. Her eyes were closed and her lips were moving.

I stared. 'What are you doing? What is all that stuff?'

Martha opened her eyes. 'Salt. I stole it from the kitchen. Sssh – I'm doing a spell.'

'You don't know any spells,' I said.

'I looked in Pokiss's books when I was supposed to be doing the washing-up,' said Martha. 'There was a spell for Finding Lost Things. Or Lost People,' she added.

She had Mum's cardigan wrapped around her. On her lap was the drawing of Mum and Dad she had done last night, only with the cannibals torn out.

'I've said all the right words,' she went on. 'I learnt them off by heart. *Cast the circle thrice around, bound and binding, finding found . . .*'

I wondered what she was expecting to happen: Mum and Dad to appear in a puff of blue smoke?

'Martha – you can't make them come back.'

Dipping her finger in her magic circle, Martha licked the salt and made a face. 'No,' she said, sadly. 'I'm a rubbish witch.'

'I expect it takes ages to learn to do it properly,' I said, to comfort her. 'A bit like playing the violin. Come on, the Grub's asleep. Show me where you found that wrapper.'

CHAPTER NINE

Martha led the way to where she had found the chocolate wrapper: down the corridor past another row of gold-framed ancestors, up and down some random steps, around a couple of corners, until she stopped and pointed at an arched door spotted with woodworm holes.

'Right there. By that door.'

I reckoned I knew where we were. 'The old tower,' I said. 'Where Uncle Dandelion lives. And where Aunt Grusilla said we shouldn't go . . .'

'Which proves that we should!' declared Martha. 'It's like when they tell you not to look in the cupboard, because that's where they've put all the Christmas presents. If you always, always, always do what you're told, you never, ever, ever find anything out. And why shouldn't we visit Uncle Dandelion? He must get lonely, shut away in that stuffy old tower all by himself. They lock him in.'

'How do you know?' I demanded.

'I was watching Pokiss,' explained Martha. 'She had to unlock the door to go through; she had two keys on a ring. She wasn't gone long. Aunt Gruesome was calling her – screeching on and on until Pokiss came back, all hissy and muttery, and went to see what she wanted. She didn't bother to lock up again. I kept quiet as a mouse; I think she forgot I was there.'

I tried the handle; it creaked open. On the other side, we found ourselves halfway up a narrow staircase winding between curved walls. The air was cold and damp; grey light filtered in through the arrow slits. I peered through one of the gaps and thought of all those long-ago archers taking aim across the moat.

Martha had already set off up the stairs. The steps were worn smooth in the middle by hundreds of years of feet going up and down them. At the top, two more suits of armour stood like sentries, holding long, sharp-tipped lances, one each side of another worm-riddled door. The key in the lock was the old-fashioned, curly sort. A second key dangled from its ring.

'Told you,' said Martha. 'Pokiss was in a hurry. She forgot to bring it down with her.'

She had turned the key and was about to push the door open.

'We should knock,' I reminded her. 'We can't just barge in, if Uncle Dandelion's in there.'

I tapped. Silence.

'Louder,' said Martha, and thumped on the door with her fist.

Still silence.

'We can go in,' said Martha. 'He's not in there.'

'Nor is Caramel,' I pointed out. 'Or why wouldn't she answer?'

Martha gave a little squeak and clutched at my arm. 'Dan, I know what Pokiss was doing up here. When she came back down, she was carrying a tape measure. Do you remember when we first arrived? She tried to measure Caramel for . . .' She stopped, biting her lip.

For her coffin.

My hand was on the door handle. 'Come on,' I said. 'We're going in.'

As the door swung open, we both held our breath. I could feel the brush and flutter of butterfly wings in my stomach.

We were at the very top of the tower. A small diamond-paned skylight let in just enough light to see by. There was no sign of Caramel. To one side was a big four-poster bed. To the other side was a desk, with an old inkwell and a bunch of feathered quills on it. In between, a high-backed wingchair faced away from us, at an angle to the fireplace. I could see an elbow in a purple silk dressing gown, and slippered feet resting on a velvet footstool. The slippers had the Bone Crest embroidered on them in gold thread.

Martha began to tiptoe forward.

'Don't,' I breathed, pulling her back.

She shook me off. 'I want to *see*.'

She crept right up to Uncle Dandelion's chair and stood looking down at him. She was there for what seemed like ages, just staring.

My skin began to prickle. I tried to keep my trainer soles silent on the stone floor as I moved. 'Is he asleep?'

'Sort of. You don't have to whisper.' Her voice sounded odd. 'You won't wake him.'

'What d'you mean?' But there was only one thing she *could* mean. 'He's not . . . dead?'

'A bit. More than a bit, actually. See for yourself.'

Half of me wanted to. Half of me didn't. I edged forward, took a deep breath and looked down at the figure in the chair.

What did Great-Uncle Dandelion look like? I couldn't tell. His face wasn't there. I was staring at bare, bleached bone: eyeholes, another hole where the nose had been, two rows of teeth. His hands were neatly folded in his purple silk lap. Lots and lots of tiny bones – although not quite as many as there should have been. One of the fingers was missing.

I took a sudden step backwards. 'He *winked* at me!'

But it was only a spider, scuttling out of an empty eye socket.

'If you're going to be sick,' said Martha, pointing at a doorway, 'there's a bathroom through there.'

It wasn't really a bathroom – more like a cupboard with a basin and a toilet in it. I wasn't sick, but my heart was beating too hard. Splashing water on my face made my eyes sting, but I could breathe properly again. Drying myself on a towel embroidered with the Bone crest, I caught sight of something that had been screwed up and tossed into the bin. Purple foil.

I pounced on it. 'Martha – look!'

Her face brightened as she smoothed out the wrapper and gave it a lick. 'It's still chocolatey.' She glanced at the wingchair. 'Dan, why have they left him here? And why are they pretending he's still alive?'

'Because of the prophecy.' I was trying to work it out. '*Here lives and breathes a true-born Bone*... They needed

Uncle Dandelion alive – at least until we got here. But I don't think you can fool a prophecy that easily: it didn't stop the Hall beginning to crumble, did it? Come on, Caramel's not here. Let's go.'

'I'm going to wash my hands.' Martha slid off the bed. 'That paper's all sticky.'

'Hurry up,' I told her. I didn't want to be left alone with Uncle Dandelion for too long.

Turning my back on him, I looked at the oil painting hanging on the wall. A man and a woman sat on opposite sides of a fireplace, in old-fashioned clothes. The woman was covered in jewels; her skirts stuck out all around her and her hair was piled up like meringue. She held a painted fan and there was a little black and white dog in her lap.

I looked at the dog. It looked back at me, with Lambkin-Wolfsnarl's bulging chocolate-button gaze.

The man wore a white curled wig, with white stockings and buckled shoes under a stiff velvet coat. His face was thin and mournful, with the same two little creases between his eyes that Dad had when he was thinking. Behind him, one hand resting on the back of his chair, stood a girl with dark hair and the same thin face; you could tell by her expression that she was bored and would rather have been somewhere else. Supposing she lost an eye and gained a moustache . . .

what would she look like? I reckoned I knew.

Down in the bottom right-hand corner of the canvas was a squiggled signature and a date in Roman numbers:

MDCCX.

You've done them at school: you can do this, I told myself.

M: that was easy – 1000.

D: what was that? 500?

C then another C: that would be 200.

X: 10

I did a bit of maths, and had my answer. There they all were: Uncle Dandelion, Aunt Grusilla and little Lambkin. And Jack. Alive and well in 1710.

More than 300 years ago.

I could feel my skin tingling, and hear the beat of my own heart. When *impossible* starts getting muddled up with *possible*, how do you know what's true or not any more?

'Martha? Hurry up, I want to show you something!'

'Wait a minute,' Martha's voice called back. 'I'm just—'

There was a creak, the rush of a water tank emptying, a gasp that turned into a scream.

Then nothing.

I hurtled into the bathroom, just in time to see the

trapdoor in front of the toilet swing silently back into place.

'Martha? *Martha!*'

I scrabbled at the floor, but it was useless. I tried to calm down, and think. Pipes were gurgling as the cistern refilled. *It opens when you flush. All you have to do is not be standing in the wrong place.* That wasn't so easy. The toilet was tucked into a corner, the handle very close to the wall. I couldn't reach. In the end I scrambled on to the wooden seat, with my knees tucked up against my ribs. One arm had to stretch across the opposite shoulder to reach the handle. I pulled; the floor creaked open in front of me.

I slid off the seat and quickly wedged a towel in the gap, stopping it from snapping shut again. 'Martha?'

'I'm *wet*.' Her voice seemed to come from a long way away. 'There's a lot of water down here. Dan, guess what – I *found* her! I found Caramel! She's all right, except she can't stop sneezing.'

'I think I'b gettig a code.' Caramel sounded hoarse. 'It's quite code and damp dowd here . . .' She broke off, in a flurry of coughing.

I was down on my knees, peering into the gaping hole. I tried shining the light from my watch into the darkness but the beam wasn't powerful enough to reach the bottom.

'They *tricked* her,' Martha informed me. 'They told her Uncle Dandelion wanted to see her, then Aunt Gruesome locked her in and left her.'

'I banged on the door and shouted for *hours*,' said Caramel. 'But nobody came. In the end, I gave up. That skeleton – no disrespect to your uncle – was giving me the heebie-jeebies, so I shut myself in the bathroom, where I couldn't see him. In the end I had to use the loo, and when I flushed it . . . well, you know what happens. It's a long way down – we're lucky it's flooded and we landed in the water. Otherwise . . .'

'Otherwise, *splat*!' said Martha. 'The other lucky thing,' she added, 'is that she had her bag with her and it was full of chocolate– but it will run out soon, so you need to rescue us before we starve.'

'Is there a door? Or a window?' I tried to remember what the tower looked like from the outside.

'I felt all the way around the walls,' said Caramel, 'but I didn't find anything. The water's dribbling in from somewhere.'

'We're sitting on a sort of ledge,' added Martha, 'but if the water keeps on coming we'll have to swim round and round and round in circles like a goldfish, until we *drown*. So it would a good thing if you rescued us *now*, Dan.'

I agreed with her – but it wasn't as easy as all that

'I'm just trying to think—' I began, then I stopped. I'd heard footsteps on the stairs. 'Someone's coming. I have to go.'

'Promise you'll come back!' I could hear panic in Martha's voice, bubbling up like the river water. 'Promise!'

'It'll be all right,' I said. You need to be careful about promises. 'I'll get you out.' *Somehow*, I added silently. There wasn't time for more. The footsteps were growing louder; I could hear voices. There was nothing I could do except pull away the towel and let the door snap shut.

I shot out of the bathroom and dived under Uncle Dandelion's bed, surprising several spiders. *Stay where you are*, I warned them. *Or Aunt Grusilla will have your legs for eyelashes.* I was only just in time.

'Did it need to be such a *big* coffin?' puffed Aunt Grusilla, as they set down the box they had been lugging between them. 'He's all bones, after all. Hurry up, Pokiss, Sir Dandelion's been sitting here long enough. Now the Heir's here, we don't need him any more; we can tidy him away.'

'Poor Pokiss,' grumbled Pokiss. 'Do this, do that, pick up bones, find a unicorn, stretch time, watch the pygmies . . . Should have kept the spiky hedgepig creature to do that.'

'It was you who said she was riddled with charms and would shrivel the Halloweeds,' Aunt Grusilla pointed out. 'So I got rid of her. Why is there a broken plate in this coffin, Pokiss? The best Bone china too.'

I held my breath, certain Pokiss would guess who had smashed that plate. To my surprise, she didn't give Martha away. 'Tss . . . sprites in the ssscrubbery,' was all she said. 'Pessky.'

Some scuffling noises followed, a bit of grunting, then a rattling sound.

'Do be *careful*, Pokiss,' nagged Aunt Grusilla. 'Watch what you're doing – look, his foot's come off. So many bones, for just one person! There – he's in. Quick, get the lid nailed down. We don't want him falling out halfway down the stairs.'

I had to get out of there before they did. If they locked the door behind them, I'd be trapped. Pokiss was hammering in nails while Aunt Grusilla stood and watched her; they both had their backs to the bed. Holding my breath, I wiggled out from under it, heading for the door. The threadbare rug was full of dust. It got up my nose . . . I was going to sneeze.

I pinched the top of my nose, hard. It's not easy, wriggling on your stomach and holding your nostrils shut at the same time. When I'd made it through the door, I stood up, pressing myself against the wall, and slipped off my trainers so they wouldn't hear me on the stairs. Then I ran.

Back in my bedroom, the Grub was stirring in its drawer.

Keep calm, I told myself, as I picked it up. *And think. There has to be a way to get them out of there.*

How, exactly?

I could hear shuffling footsteps, Aunt Grusilla's heavy breathing, then a grunt and a soft hiss from Pokiss. Uncle Dandelion was on his way downstairs.

Jack. She'll help. I'd meet her in the maze at three. Until then, there was nothing I could do.

'Pokiss has gone to Witches' Cross,' announced Aunt Grusilla, at lunch. 'She has left us a pie.'

I wished she hadn't: it had a lot of little beaks sticking out of it.

'The cat has been bringing in sparrows again. Where's the girl?' asked Aunt Grusilla, cutting into the pie and handing me a plateful of grey-ish water and wet feathers.

'Martha doesn't feel well. She doesn't want any lunch.' Looking at what was in front of me, nor did I.

'What's the matter with her?' Aunt Grusilla sounded suspicious.

'She has a headache. And a stomach ache. And a sore throat.' I listed symptoms at random. 'And spots.' *Better stop there: if you make her any iller, she'll be dead.*

'Is she coming out in lumps at all?' asked Aunt Grusilla hopefully. 'It sounds like the Black Death. People aren't dying like they used to; we'll get some customers at last, if the Plague's back. *Sneezes and diseases, germs are what pleases.* But you must stay away from her, Dandelion. We have to keep you safe. Until tomorrow.'

'Tomorrow?' *Halloween.*

'It's a special day for you.' Aunt Grusilla removed a bit of feather that had got stuck between her teeth. 'The first day of your future. A very special future.'

I shuffled a beak and a little clawed foot to the edge of my plate. I'd never thought very much about the Future; I'd always been happy in the Present – until the cannibals. 'I might be an entomologist,' I said. 'Like Mum and Dad. When I grow up.'

'Silly boy.' Aunt Grusilla's chins wobbled with laughter. 'Who said anything about growing up?'

The rain kept falling, out of a sky the colour of pencil lead. Aunt Grusilla said I could spend the afternoon in my room, studying the Family Tree.

'This is your history, Dandelion,' she announced,

unrolling it. It was written on a long scroll of paper, crispy with age and stained the colour of tea. 'I shall come back later and test you, so pay attention.'

The tree began with Sir Lyon and Lady Clotilda. After them stretched a long line of Dandelion Bones, all getting married and having more little Dandelions. Right at the bottom, a Sir Dandelion Perceval Bone got married to Grusilla Dorcas Gosling-Shrike. They had one daughter: Jacobina Berengaria Bone. *Jack.* I peered at the date, scratched in tiny numbers beside her name. 1699. Which meant that in the portrait in the tower she would have been eleven, the same age as me, and now she'd be three hundred and . . .

That's impossible. It isn't true. How can it be?

The afternoon dragged on. The Grub kept moaning and dribbling, wanting to be picked up. Keeping an eye out for Aunt Grusilla or Pokiss, I carried it to the end of the corridor and tried the door to the tower. It was locked. I thought of Martha and Caramel, shivering and sneezing in their damp dungeon, and wondered where Pokiss kept the key.

By half past two, the Grub was rubbing its eyes, ready for another nap. Relieved, I pulled the string on the musical mouse. It would be much easier to slip out to meet Jack without it.

Downstairs, the stopped hands on the grandfather clock told the right time for once. It was ten minutes to three and I was on my way out of the front doors when the smell of dead things – roses and rats – filled my nose. Aunt Grusilla. *Oh no. Not now!*

'Dandelion? Where are you going? Not out in this rain, I hope! We don't want you catching your death of cold.'

I was racking my brains for an excuse – something that would make her let me go – when hooves clattered in the courtyard. A dripping Pokiss dragged on Death's reins, pulling him up to a steaming, stamping halt. I tried not to look at the fluffy slippers in the stirrups, her soft maggoty-white toes.

'It doesn't take that long to buy a flower pot and a bag of potting compost,' complained Aunt Grusilla. 'What have you been doing?'

'Ssshopping.' Sliding off Death's back, Pokiss heaved down a saddle bag. 'Eye of newt, toe of frog. Wool of bat. Fillet of fenny snake for your supper. Nice . . . sss.' She saw me looking at the bag and whisked it out of sight; not before I'd seen what looked a lot like a box of cornflakes and a packet of chocolate Hobnobs. 'And,' she added, 'a unicorn.'

Aunt Grusilla clapped her hands together. 'At last. Where did you find it?'

'Nickett and Floggit's Sssecond-hand Bargains. Ssspecial offer, today only. Quality pure-bred Monoceros Rarissimus. One careful owner. Cash on delivery.'

'A second-hand unicorn?' Aunt Grusilla frowned. 'Are you sure Mr Nickett and Mr Floggit are to be trusted? Those cockatrice talons they sold you last year looked very like chicken claws to me. And the dragon scales smelt distinctly fishy. They didn't cure that wart, did they?'

'Nothing wrong with their asses' milk and tincture of crocodile tears,' said Pokiss stiffly. 'Can't have been, or you'd still have that toe fungus. Beggars can't be choosers. Unicorns don't grow on trees.'

'It had better be in working order and produce some dung,' grumbled Aunt Grusilla, 'or I shall want my money back. Go and make room in the stables, Pokiss. I shall go upstairs and count out some guineas.'

It was easy after that. Neither of them noticed me slip past the lion and the unicorn, out into the rain. It was three minutes to three.

CHAPTER TEN

The sky was dark and angry. The rain fell in cold needles rather than drops. As I pushed through the overgrown walls of the maze, the spiky yew branches lashed out at my face and arms. My trainers were leaking, my sodden socks cold and clammy against my skin but I hardly noticed; I was in a hurry. I had to keep one eye on the wet grass, watching for the glint of gold to show me the way. I missed a turning and came up against a dead end. *I'll be late. Jack won't wait.* As I retraced my steps, the dark hedges closed in on me, arching over my head. *Did she bother to come at all?*

'*Falafel,*' said a voice above my head. '*French fries.*

Fromage frais. Fish cakes. Fruit basket.'

I breathed a sigh of relief. If the Beak was here, so was Jack.

She was leaning against the statue of Venus, eating monkey nuts. 'Neptune's armpit, you look about as cheerful as a squashed squid!' she remarked. 'What's wrong?'

'Everything!' I said. 'Martha's fallen down a hole in the toilet. Caramel's down there too – she's been down there two days and she's got a cold – and all they have to eat is chocolate and Pokiss has the key and the water's getting in and Boy told me about the flooding and the bones being washed white as snow – and I can't get them out and I don't know what to do . . .'

'Slow down,' advised Jack, as I ran out of breath. 'And begin at the beginning.'

When I'd explained, rather more clearly, she seemed to be mostly interested in how the trapdoor worked.

'My father's design,' she guessed. 'He liked things that worked with cogs and levers. He invented the Pump-Driven Corset-Lacer for my mother, and a Steam-Powered Hair-Curler. She never could stand the idea of Time always ticking *forwards*, so he spent years working on a Tick-less Backwards Clock. It was powered by mice, running in a wheel, but they kept turning round and going the wrong way so he had to give up. Most of the mice escaped. One of them got into Mother's hair and she had hysterics. My father had to invent a Mechanical Mouse-Mincer. It's true,' she added, offering me a nut, 'about the dungeon flooding. It always happens when the river rises.'

'Martha's not a brilliant swimmer,' I said urgently. 'She can only do the frog stroke and she keeps forgetting not to sink. And there's no way out.'

'Actually,' said Jack, 'there is. Most prisoners never found it – not unless the water took them high enough – but halfway up the wall you can get through a gap, into a tunnel. It leads to the kitchen. The story goes that a long-ago Bone – the fierce sort – didn't like the man his daughter wanted to marry. He threw the boy in the dungeon, but his daughter wasn't the sort to give up. She dug a tunnel and rescued him. Useful for us,' she said, cracking a nut between her teeth. 'The entrance is in the kitchen, but you'll need me with you, to show you the way. There's a whole labyrinth of tunnels down there. On your own, you could get lost and never be seen again. Our best chance is to do it by night. You're in the Heir's Bedroom, I suppose? Leave the window open. When the lights go out and all's quiet, I'll come for you.' She was already turning to go.

'Wait a minute,' I said. 'I saw the portrait in Uncle Dandelion's tower. And your name in the Family Tree.

I saw the dates. Jack – *how old are you?*'

Jack shrugged. 'To be honest,' she admitted, 'I've rather lost count.'

'You *can't* be three hundred and something,' I accused her. 'Like the Family Tree says. That's impossible.'

'Possible; impossible. It's not always that simple.' Jack sat down on Venus's marble foot. 'Sometimes you can turn one into the other, if you really, really want to. My mother really, really wanted to live for ever. She couldn't make it happen – but she found somebody who could.'

I stared at her. 'Who . . . ?' But I already knew the answer. 'Pokiss! She's a witch – a proper one – *isn't she?*'

'We were famous for witches in these parts, once upon a time,' said Jack. 'They used to hang them at Witches' Cross. The last person condemned to die there was a girl named Eliza Fishblood. Nobody had ever bothered about her much – until the day her neighbour's pig died . . . Then the rumours started to spread: Eliza could turn herself into a black crow and fly; she could summon demons down her chimney; she kept a cauldron for boiling babies in. When they'd scared themselves silly, the villagers marched to Eliza's cottage and dragged her out. She confessed to it all.'

'Why?' I was puzzled. 'If it wasn't true?'

'Probably because they'd pulled all her toenails out,' said Jack grimly. 'And they were about to start on her fingers. It would have been her teeth next. The Witchfinders had their own ways of making people confess. The whole village took the day off to see her hanged at Witches' Cross.'

I shivered, thinking of the rope dangling from the Hanging Tree, the terrified girl and the crowd of people, waiting to watch her die.

'But,' said Jack, 'at the very last moment, with the noose already around Eliza's neck, a coach and horses arrived at the gallop. Eliza was bundled in and the door slammed shut on her. The coach had a crest on its panels – a lion and a unicorn, with two crossed swords. It wheeled round and set off back the way it had come – towards Daundelyon Hall. The villagers chased after it but the portcullis came slamming down before they had time to cross the drawbridge. They never saw Eliza Fishblood again.'

'What happened to her?'

Jack snapped a peanut shell in half. 'There was trouble up at the Hall – Sir Dandelion was growing old and had no son. Just a daughter, but she didn't count. His only heir was a distant nephew, who would take his place when he died. This did not suit his wife, who liked being Lady of Daundelyon Hall. She struck a bargain with Eliza Fishblood: she would save her from the hangman's rope. In return, Eliza would use her magic to keep affairs as they were, so nothing need change at the Hall. Ever.'

I frowned. 'So Eliza *was* a witch?'

Jack shrugged. 'Whatever she was in the beginning, now it was her only chance. You can learn to be anything you want to be, if you work at it hard enough. Eliza worked so hard it drained the life out of her. She shrivelled away until all that was left was . . .'

'. . . Pokiss,' I said. I thought of her empty, dishwater eyes and colourless, cobwebby hair, her damaged toes. I felt sorry for Eliza, but it was harder to feel sorry for what she had become.

Jack nodded. 'Night and day, Eliza studied her books, her *grimoires*. When she found what she was looking for – a way to hold off Age, and Death – she began experimenting. On mice and rats and birds. Then on Lambkin and Boy.' She paused and I saw her nine fingers curl into fists. 'And then,' she went on, 'on All Hallows' Eve after my fourteenth birthday, she experimented on me.'

'A finger . . .' I breathed. 'She took your finger!'

Jack nodded. 'They watched me all the time, afterwards, waiting to see what happened. When they were sure that it had worked, that I wasn't getting any older, Pokiss took more fingers: her own and my mother's – and my father's. As long as they could keep Sir Dandelion alive, it didn't matter that there was no Heir.'

'What does Pokiss *do* with the fingers?' I wasn't positive I wanted to know, but I couldn't help asking.

Jack shook her head. 'I never found out. They wouldn't tell me. All I knew was that I was trapped: stuck at the Hall, stuck being fourteen, and nothing was going to change. Not ever. I knew I had to run away. I'd never been further than Witches' Cross before, but I followed the river to the coast – disguised as a boy, in case they bothered to come looking for me. I didn't care which ship I boarded, or where it was going, as long as it was far away from Daundelyon Hall.

'When we were captured by pirates, I joined their crew. They never guessed I was a girl. Pirates don't like sailing with a woman on board. The years went by. I outlived more men than I can count and ended up as captain of my own ship – Black Jack, Terror of the High Seas, that was me. We had some exciting times, the *Goose* and I – sea monsters and the smell of gunpowder and pirate gold.'

'What made you give it up?' I wondered.

'The High Seas aren't what they used to be,' said Jack regretfully. 'And everything has to come to an end. My crew helped me bring *The Goose* home to roost. I paid them all handsomely and we went our separate ways.' She sighed, twisting the end of her llama moustache around her finger. 'They'll all be long gone by now: just names on a gravestone, or bones on the sea floor. That's the worst part – watching everyone around you grow old and pass on. You're always the one left behind.'

'Ordinary life would seem a bit dull,' I guessed, 'after being a pirate. What did you do instead?'

'Oh – everything,' said Jack, yawning. 'I climbed mountains, dived for pearls, crossed deserts and icecaps. I can speak seventeen languages, play twenty-three musical instruments and recite the longest poem in the world forwards or backwards. I can read Ancient Egyptian hieroglyphics or walk a tightrope blindfold while juggling a dozen eggs. I had plenty of time for it all. But it can't go on for ever.' Jack stood up, scattering peanut shells. 'Everybody has the right to a Beginning *and* an End. Pokiss and my mother stole my End. I'm here to get it back. I want my finger.'

I tried to imagine living for ever. 'All those things you don't have to be afraid of,' I said. 'Plane crashes and poisonous spiders and deadly diseases and asteroids landing on you . . .'

'There are other things to be afraid of,' said Jack. 'Like being alone . . . But it will be different now. I'm glad you came, Dan. Forever's a lot more fun with two.'

It took me a moment to understand her. 'You mean ... they're going to take my finger too?'

'*Here lives and breathes a true-born Bone, Or these walls crumble stone by stone,*' recited Jack. 'They're already crumbling. My father's dead, isn't he?'

I nodded, a bit uncomfortable about that. I didn't want to tell her that I'd seen his skeleton, in dressing gown and slippers, still sitting in his chair.

'It's all right,' Jack assured me. 'I hardly knew him – fathers didn't pay their children much attention in my day. But my mother won't let the Hall fall down around her if she can help it. She's been there so long, she's become part of it. If it were to crumble, she'd crumble with it. So – she needs to keep you safe.'

'But they wouldn't do it *now*. They'll wait until I'm older, won't they?' My skin felt clammy. 'Aunt Grusilla doesn't like children. Why would she want to keep me eleven?'

'Because you'll do as you're told,' said Jack. 'You won't have any choice. You'll be in her power. For ever.'

For ever sounded like a very long time. I tried to imagine it. Never growing up, never growing old, never having to think about those things that adults fuss over, like bills and bald patches and parking tickets and prime ministers.

Then I thought of Martha and the Grub growing up, taller than me, older than me, then really, *really* old, then not being there at all. I'd be left by myself in a world full of people who weren't even born yet.

'No,' I said. 'I'd rather keep my finger.'

'You don't have to make your mind up right now. At least think about it,' suggested Jack.

I stared at her. 'You *want* me to get my finger chopped off?'

She shrugged. 'I didn't say that. But how many people get the chance to live for ever? Do you really want to grow up, and get old, and not be here any more? You don't have to stay at Daundelyon Hall. Let them do it, then run away – like I did. Don't you want to see what the world is like in another hundred years? A thousand years?'

'You've been trying to get your finger *back*,' I reminded her. '*Everybody has the right to a Beginning and an End.* That's what you said. Now you want them to steal my End, like they stole yours. And what about Martha and the Grub? I promised I'd look after them.'

'They won't need looking after for long,' said Jack. 'They'll grow up and have families of their own. They'll grow old, and then a bit older and then ... they won't need you any more. I need you more than they do,' she added gruffly. 'Having all the time in the world – it gets boring when you're all by yourself. We could have adventures, Dan – you and I.'

I didn't know what to say. My head was whirling. I'm not the world's most decisive person – it's hard enough knowing if I want jam or peanut butter on my toast. To live for ever, or not: that had to be the biggest decision I'd ever make. 'I'll have to think about it.'

'You don't have long,' Jack warned me. 'It's Halloween tomorrow. If there's witchery to be done, that's when it will happen. Go back now, before they miss you. Don't let them suspect you've met me. Let my mother think you're the Heir she's always wanted. I'll come for you tonight, and we'll release the prisoners. Expect me after midnight.'

I had to pass the Glass House on my way back, its white frame rising out of the ground like a giant ribcage. I didn't mean to go in. It was because of the cat. I saw it through the glass, mewing and scratching to be let out. When I pushed open the door, it wound around my legs, purring.

'I don't think you're meant to be in here,' I told it. 'Where's Boy?'

The only sign of life was a butterfly, beating its wings against the glass. On a trestle table, a big geranium dropped its petals – the colour of blood. Next to it, a row of little pots all had green sprigs in them. Boy had been taking cuttings; I'd watched Dad doing it in the greenhouse at home.

'Easy,' he'd said. 'You snip a piece off the big plant, pop it in some earth and – abracadabra, just like magic! – it puts down roots and you've got a new baby plant. Just imagine if you could do that with people . . .'

It was so quiet you could almost hear the plants breathing. The air smelt of damp earth – and something else, a bit like raw meat. A bunch of tiny fruits, like beads, brushed against my cheek. I picked one and ate it, but the sourness made my nose wrinkle. The sharp edge of a palm leaf sliced at my cheek.

With the cat stalking ahead of me, I wandered further in, through a thicket of bamboo. I tried not to step on the dead. Some of the stones had been there so long they had sunk into the earth; all you could see of them were their curved rims like giants' toenail clippings. Others leant at angles, green with moss or blotched with lichen, like slices of mouldy bread, the writing on them rubbed out by Time.

The butterfly fluttered past me and the cat went after it, leaping on to a marble tomb where a man and woman lay side by side, carved out of pale stone. Their eyes were closed, as if they were sleeping, and their hands were crossed neatly on their chests. I'd guessed who they were, even before I'd scraped away the moss and read the inscription cut into the side:

Sir Lyon de Beaune
also
his wife, Lady Clotilda

I shivered, thinking of the bones lying inside. The cat twitched its ears, tuned in to sounds I couldn't hear. When it jumped off the tomb and disappeared through a curtain of hanging vines, I followed – and almost fell into an open grave.

I teetered on the edge, catching wildly at branches to save myself as the ground gaped at my feet.

I stared down into the rectangle of newly-dug earth. The skeleton lying at the bottom of it was wrapped in a black tailcoat, with a little posy of wild flowers wilting in the buttonhole. I'd seen those flowers just yesterday; they had been freshly picked for Bessie Fleaspoon's funeral. The toothless skull smiled up at me from under its shabby, slightly squashed top hat.

It was Boy.

If you have a mum who works in a museum, you grow up knowing a few things about skeletons. Things like: it takes a long time to be one. Much, much longer than a day. *So what had happened to Boy?*

A fly was buzzing around a flower with blotched salami-coloured petals. Was that where the meaty smell was coming from? As I sniffed it, something moved, very close to my nose. I straightened up, taking a step backwards. The fly had disappeared. A muffled *zzzzz* came from the end of a green stalk, where clam-shaped jaws had just snapped shut. I'd seen Venus Fly-traps before, dinky little things living in a saucer. This was different . . .

Behind me I heard a rustle, then a yowl. Half a yowl, cut off very suddenly, in the middle.

I spun round. A monster of a plant was swaying in front of me, tendrils rippling like serpents. Its leaves were ragged and laced with holes. It looked angry and *hungry*, as if it had just caught its first proper meal in weeks.

A tuft of grey fur floated downwards. A tail stuck out from between fleshy green lips. *The Cabbages* . . . who grew in graveyard soil and ate sausages if they had to, but would rather have fresh meat . . .

A muffled *mee-yowl* snapped me out of my daze.

'No!' I shouted at the plant. 'Let it go!'

I made a leap for the cat's tail and hung on. The Cabbage tugged one way. I tugged the other. When the plant reared suddenly backwards, I lost my grip. I was clutching at a nearby gravestone to stop myself from falling when the cat flew suddenly over my head, in a shower of green slime-gobs. The plant had spat it out.

Get out. Get out of here! As the cat bolted, dripping and terrified, for the open door I turned to follow. It was no good: they were all around me now, snaking and slithering. Trails of digestive juice dribbled from their jaws. They were drooling, like dogs waiting for a biscuit.

And the biscuit was me. I knew it with horrible stomach-squeezing certainty. The plant had only let the cat go because I looked meatier, and tastier, and less likely to give it hairballs. The food chain had flipped upside down.

I was about to be Vegetables' Soup.

Panic exploded inside me, not leaving room to breathe. As tendrils came twisting and twining towards me, I looked around for a weapon. A garden hose lay in loops on the ground at my feet. I grabbed at it. There was a nozzle on the end, with a trigger. As the biggest Cabbage reached out, I squeezed the trigger and hoped...

I was in luck. The hose was connected and the tap had been left on. A jet of water came shooting out like a crystal laser beam, better than any water gun. *Aim. Fire.* The plants drew back, bruised by the high-pressure stream.

'Don't like it, do you? So what are you going to do about it, hey?' I began to feel braver. I was Sir Lyon de Beaune, swinging my sword and scaring off the enemy. Above my head was a hanging basket, spilling a waterfall of flowers. I yanked it from its bracket, whirling it by the chain, around and around my head, scattering earth and petals. Lion's Tooth, Lion's Paw. The Cabbages could rustle as spitefully as they liked; they weren't getting near me.

Slice, slash, whirl. I began backing towards the door. Slime-oozy jaws craned after me, but the plants' roots kept them anchored; they could only stretch so far. A few more steps and I'd be out of their reach.

'You're not frightening *me*,' I told them. 'Back off, or I'll turn you all into *salad*!'

Then I fell over.

I must have hit my head on the edge of a gravestone as I went down. For a moment, all I could do was lie there – like Sir Lyon on his tomb – staring up at the rain battering the glass roof. Dazed, I turned my head sideways to see what had tripped me. A long, creeping stalk . . .

Heart kicking, I rolled away from it but it didn't move. Its leaves were limp, dull and dead. Very dead. Its stem had been chopped right through. I could see the damp stain where the sap had trickled from the wound.

I thought of Aunt Grusilla and the Dent de Lyon. *Snicker snack...*

I felt a tug on my leg. The other plants had caught up with me. Fleshy tendrils were coiling around my ankle. Raising the hose, I aimed the nozzle and squeezed the trigger. Nothing happened. The fall must have jerked it loose from the tap. I struggled to sit up, trying to hit out with the hanging basket, but more tendrils caught hold of the chain, pulling it away from me. The stench of rotting meat hung over me, making my stomach heave. I looked up, straight into the jaws of death by vegetable. There were two of them, their juices bubbling and frothing in happy anticipation. A third, smaller one was already nipping at my legs. I was doomed.

Apparently, getting eaten ran in the family.

I shut my eyes.

CHAPTER ELEVEN

'Tssss!'

Fingers clawed at my neck, pulling me backwards. The plants had me by the feet, pulling me forwards. I felt like a Christmas cracker. Any minute now, there'd be a loud bang and I'd come apart . . .

'Ssstop it!'

The plants were backing off; my feet were free. Pokiss hauled me up by my collar.

'Ssstupid!'

She was shaking me, but I didn't care. It was just nice not to be dissolving into a puddle of slime. She marched me out of the Cabbages' reach, kicking at my ankles if I stopped or stumbled. When she let go, I crumpled up. My legs felt like Bone Jelly. A shape darkened the doorway.

'No damage, I hope?' Aunt Grusilla shook the raindrops off her umbrella, showering Lambkin who was at her heels, already looking like a drowned rat

Pokiss sniffed. 'Rough boy. Nasssty.'

'I am disappointed in you, Dandelion,' declared Aunt Grusilla. 'I can't have you hurting my Halloweeds. Did your parents not teach you to respect Nature?'

'There's nothing *natural* about those things.' I shuddered. 'They nearly ate the cat, then they tried to eat *me*.'

'All living organisms must feed,' said Aunt Grusilla. 'The Halloweeds have been nurtured from cuttings. They are very precious and must be kept alive – at any cost.'

'One of them's dead,' I said. 'You chopped it down.'

Aunt Grusilla shut her umbrella with a snap. 'Dead wood,' she said briskly. 'I put it out of its misery. It will soon be replaced.' She looked at Boy's row of geranium cuttings, and the pair of garden snippers lying beside them. 'Can't we do it now, Pokiss?'

Pokiss's dishwater eyes flickered. 'Too soon. Tomorrow. All Hallows' Eve.'

My brain was still un-fuzzing itself from shock. 'Do what?'

'You are the luckiest boy in the world,' Aunt Grusilla informed me. 'We have very special plans for you. Do you know much about gardening, Dandelion?'

I wiped a globule of Cabbage-slime off my jeans. 'I used to help Dad sometimes.'

'Then you will know that a good gardener must sometimes cut part of a plant away. Pruning it helps it stay healthy and strong–' grabbing at my hand, she forced it down on the table, squeezing each of my fingers in turn – 'And if you choose your cuttings carefully, they will put down roots and grow.' She picked up the snippers, snapping them open and shut. 'Just one finger, Dandelion. There are people who would give a great deal more than that, for what we are offering you. A Halloweed of your very own.'

'Those things grow from *fingers*?' Eyeing the snippers, I tried to snatch my hand back but Aunt Grusilla held on to it.

'Plants can live for thousands of years, Dandelion. With the right care and attention, there is no reason why they can't live for ever. And for as long as your Halloweed flourishes, so will you, without ever growing a day older.'

'What happens if they die?' But I already knew the answer. I'd seen what happened. 'Boy . . .' I drew a shuddering breath. '*You* did it! You cut down his plant and you *killed* him!'

'It was his job to look after the plants,' said Aunt Grusilla coldly. 'But he let your uncle's die, and refused to feed the others properly. People should do as they are told. You do as you're told, don't you, Dandelion? You're a good boy. *Aren't* you?'

Her ringed fingers dug into my wrist, hurting me.

'Mmm,' I said, shifting. 'But couldn't we wait until I'm older?' I suggested. 'I'm only eleven. I don't need a Halloweed yet.'

'Whatever's the point of growing you twice as large?' said Aunt Grusilla. 'You'll only eat more. And Daundelyon Hall depends upon you, now your uncle is gone. We can't risk anything happening to you. You may choose your finger,' she added graciously. 'Which one will you say goodbye to?'

I didn't want to say goodbye to any of them. After eleven years together, I was attached to them all. 'No!' Pulling my hand free, I clenched my fists. 'They're mine.'

'Ungrateful child!' Aunt Grusilla's chins quivered with annoyance. 'You're not afraid of one little *snip-snap*, are you? Come along, Dandelion. Be a man.'

But that was just it. If I let them do it, I never *would* be a man. I'd be eleven for ever. Martha would grow up; so would the Grub. I thought of them both bigger than me, bossing me around . . .

Then I remembered Jack's warning. *Let her think you're the Heir she's always wanted.*

'I'm not afraid.' It was easier to sound like I meant it if I didn't look at the snippers. 'I'll choose my finger. I'll have to think about it. It may take me quite a long time.'

'Dear little Dandelion!' Aunt Grusilla pinched my cheek. I just stopped myself from jerking my head away. 'I knew you would be sensible. Run along, then. As a treat, Pokiss will make you some miced buns for supper.'

'Tssss.'

I heard the soft hiss and felt those dishwater eyes on my back as I turned and ran.

Luckily, Pokiss had run out of mice. Aunt Grusilla was annoyed, and ordered her to put more cheese in the Mechanical Mouse Mincers.

'I like cheese,' I said hopefully, but I got snails' eggs on toast instead, while Aunt Grusilla gobbled her fillet of snake in fungus gravy. The toast was crunchy and I was too busy worrying about Martha and Caramel, and what time Jack would come, to pay much attention to the little jellied balls sliding down my throat.

The Grub didn't want to go into its drawer that night. It thrashed about and threw its bottle on the floor.

Reaching for it under my bed, where it had rolled, I found one of Martha's pens: blueberry-scented purple. I drew faces on each of my fingers, waggling them at the Grub to make it laugh. Smiley face, smiley face, smiley face, angry thumb – then a crying face on the little finger. Would chopping off a little finger hurt less than a bigger one? I didn't want to think about it. *Jack,* I thought, *come soon . . .*

Wrestling with the last nappy of the day, I realized that when Jack and I went down into the tunnels we would have to leave the Grub behind. Before popping the poppers on its sleepsuit, I picked up Martha's purple pen and drew a blueberry-scented eye on its tummy where nobody would see it. *Keep watch while I'm gone. Let it be safe. Please.*

There was no point getting into pyjamas: I would stay up, and wait for Jack. The Grub's eyes had closed at last. I stood by the open window, listening to the drumming of the rain and wondering how high the water had risen in the dungeon. The wind blew in, spattering me with raindrops. I was shivering – and my bed looked warm. I kicked off my shoes and climbed in. No danger of falling asleep: I was too worried about Martha. Much too worried. Much, much . . .

The next thing I knew, someone was shaking my shoulder. 'Sleepyhead! Wake up!'

'Jack?' Heavy with sleep, my eyes didn't want to open. 'Is it after midnight?'

'It's almost dawn, you dozy boy.' The voice was not Jack's. 'It's Halloween. Your special day!'

I was wide awake now. Aunt Grusilla was bending over me, still in her nightgown (size Walrus, Extra Large) and white nightcap. Without her mouse eyebrows, spider-leg lashes and beetle-juice blush, her face was pale and bald. I struggled up on my pillows. *Martha!* How long had I been asleep for? *Where was Jack? Why hadn't she come?*

'Hurry up, Dandelion.' Aunt Grusilla peeled the covers off me. She didn't seem to notice that I'd gone to bed in my jeans. 'Pokiss is waiting. It is Time.'

'Time for what?' I knew the answer. The back of my neck tingled and I felt something like the flapping of bat wings in my stomach.

'Put your shoes on,' ordered Aunt Grusilla. 'We're going out to the Glass House. Pokiss is sharpening the snippers.'

'Can't we do it later?' I pleaded. 'It's not properly Halloween yet. Not until tonight.'

'Nonsense,' said Aunt Grusilla. 'Dawn is the perfect time for a new beginning, the start of a new life: a new

Halloweed.'

As she dragged me out into the corridor I looked back at the Grub, asleep on its stomach with Martha's iguanodon pressed against its cheek. I hoped the Eye would keep it safe.

Aunt Grusilla towed me down the stairs. The front doors stood open; outside the darkness was fading into the milky light of dawn. There was something strange about the silence. I realized what it was: the rain had stopped.

You could just run away. Aunt Grusilla wouldn't catch you. Hide in the Deepness. Find Jack.

But how could I run away from Martha and the Grub?

And Jack didn't care. She wanted me to lose a finger, so she didn't have to spend the rest of forever being alone...

It was too late anyway: Pokiss was standing in the doorway, blocking my escape. In one hand she held a little flowerpot, full to the brim with earth. From her other hand dangled something sharp and silvery: the newly-sharpened snippers. My stomach-bats flapped harder.

Between them, Aunt Grusilla and Pokiss bundled me downstairs. The front doors stood open; I shivered, not just because of the cold. *Oh Jack, why didn't you come?*

Then something did come. Ghostly in the grey light, it trotted through the gatehouse: a white beast with a single horn. We all froze. I heard Pokiss's sharp hiss.

'*Unicorn!*' breathed Aunt Grusilla.

There was something familiar about that unicorn. I'd seen it before – grazing in the Deepness, beneath Jack's ship. I looked at its spiralled horn and remembered the piece of driftwood in the captain's cabin, waiting to be carved . . . As we all stared at it, the 'unicorn' lifted its tail and deposited something on the ground: a string of hay-flecked balls. I sniffed. A smell was hanging on the air.

'*Dung!*' Aunt Grusilla was ecstatic. 'Pokiss – pick it up! Lower the portcullis! Don't let it go away!'

The stillness broke. Pokiss dived for the gatehouse while Aunt Grusilla flung herself at the unicorn, in a sort of rugby tackle. Kicking out its back legs, it galloped away from her.

YEE-HAW! YEE-HAW!

Pokiss stopped in her tracks, halfway to the portcullis. 'Doesn't sssound like unicorn . . .'

'How do you know?' panted Aunt Grusilla, chasing after the Barnacle. 'I don't care what it *sounds* like. I just want more of that dung! Don't stand there gawping, Pokiss – help me catch the beast!'

I felt a touch on my shoulder. Jack separated herself from the shadows. 'Come on,' she whispered. 'We have to get into the kitchen.'

'I thought you weren't coming,' I told her, as we slipped back indoors.

'Pokiss was still awake at midnight, up to her tricks,' said Jack. 'I realized we were going to need a distraction. It takes time to carve a unicorn horn. And the Barnacle wasn't too keen on wearing it.'

'Suppose they catch him?' I asked.

'They won't,' said Jack. 'After all those years of giving donkey rides, he doesn't like people very much. Don't worry: he can look after himself.'

In the kitchen, she went straight over to the black beam with the evil little goblin faces carved into it. 'Where are you?' she muttered, taking a torch from her pocket and shining its light over them. 'There you are!' A goblin with bulging eyes was sticking its tongue out at her. 'Excuse *me*,' said Jack, and tweaked its tongue to the left. As it moved, there was a groaning sound and the wall shifted. Jack stepped through the gap, with me at her heels.

The torchlight flickered over a flight of narrow steps; there was nowhere to go but down. By the time we reached the bottom, the door had creaked shut again behind us. The air – what there was of it – smelt damp and a bit ratty, and the walls felt slimy against my fingers. I tried not to brush against them but it was difficult; if I shrank away from one, I bumped into the other. My feet were wet. The torchlight glinted off water; quite a lot of water. There was a sudden skitter and a squeak; something ran past me, going the other way.

'Mind your head,' warned Jack. 'The ceiling gets lower. And stay close.'

Soon we were crawling, my wet jeans clammy against my legs. Jack carried the torch between her teeth, like a pirate's dagger; I didn't like the wavering shadows it made. When she stopped suddenly, I didn't notice in time and went into the back of her.

'Mmmph. Sorry.'

'Ssssh!' She had taken the torch out of her mouth. 'Listen!'

I could hear scrabbling sounds. I don't mind rats, but I prefer it when they're not running over my hands in dark tunnels. Then – very loudly and definitely – somebody sneezed.

'Caramel!'

'Dan? Is that you?'

It didn't take us long to reach her – or rather, to reach the mound of rubble that blocked the tunnel in between us.

'Roof's caved in,' said Jack, moving the torch beam over it. 'We're going to have to shift it.'

The tunnel had widened just enough for me to crawl up beside Jack. 'Caramel? We were coming to rescue you! How did you get out?'

'The water came in over our ledge.' Caramel's voice was muffled. 'We had to swim. Martha got tired of the frog stroke and was hanging on to the wall when she found a gap leading into this tunnel, then we got stuck.' As she stopped for another explosive sneeze, we could hear the rubble rattling. 'I've moved a lot of it,' she added hopefully. 'If you work on it from that side, we'll soon be through.'

'But,' I said, '*where's Martha?*'

'She went to look for another way out.' Caramel sounded anxious. 'The tunnel branches off down another passage behind us. She said she wouldn't be long, but . . . Dan, she's been gone for *ages*.'

I thought of Martha lost, somewhere in the maze of dark tunnels. I thought of rushing water and broken ankles and collapsing ceilings and red-eyed rats the size of cats. 'Why did you let her go on her own?'

I heard Caramel's sigh. 'You'll understand,' she said sadly, 'when you see where she went.'

Lying propped on our elbows, Jack and I pulled at chunks of brick, piece by piece, until our fingers bled.

It was taking too long. I tried not to think about the mass of earth above me and the stream of cold water trickling past me. *Aphid. Bean weevil. Carrot fly.* Insects always calmed me down. *Dagger moth. Eye gnat. Furniture beetle* . . .

I let out a squawk as something scuttled up my back and over my shoulder. Jack shone the torch at its departing bottom and long bald tail as it vanished into the rubble. A moment later Caramel let out an answering squawk the other side.

'If Mr Rat can get through,' said Jack, 'then so can we.'

She was right. It wasn't long after that before Caramel's white face appeared, smeary with rubble dust, her wet hair plastered to her head. As soon as the gap was big enough, I wriggled through to her side. Jack passed me the torch and I moved the beam over the tunnel walls.

'Where did Martha go?'

'There!' Caramel pointed to where a low brick arch, like a downturned mouth, marked the entrance to another passage.

I forgave her, straight away, for letting Martha go on her own. Martha would have wiggled through easily; I'd fit, just; Caramel wouldn't stand a chance.

'That's what comes of eating too much chocolate,'

she said sadly. 'You don't fit through holes when you need to. If I ever get out of here, I'll just eat lettuce.'

There wasn't room to hug her, so I gave her a pat. 'Don't,' I told her. 'Anyway, I don't think any grown-up could fit through there, not even Jack.' I took a deep breath. 'Somebody has to go after Martha – it's going to have to be me.'

I sort of hoped that somebody would come up with a better plan. Nobody did.

'If you're sure,' said Jack, not giving me time to say that I wasn't. 'We can't have Caramel sneezing like a herd of elephants all over the place – she'll bring the rest of the roof down. I'll take her as far as the temple in the maze, then I'll come back for you. Don't forget to mark your way.' Digging in her pocket, she passed me a handful of her gold coins.

'Oh!' said Caramel. 'Chocolate?'

'Spanish doubloons,' said Jack. 'Sorry.'

'Where does it go?' I asked doubtfully, looking at the tunnel.

'I don't know,' admitted Jack. 'Maybe towards the Glass House . . .'

'No!' I was already shivering; now my blood ran even colder. 'Not there! Jack, *that's where the fingers are*! They plant them and they grow into these huge, horrible Halloweeds. They feed off bodies, dead or alive – they tried to eat me, but Pokiss rescued me. As long as your Halloweed's alive, so are you.'

Jack was gripping my arm; I saw the four fingers of her other hand curling into her palm. 'How many of these Halloweeds did you see? Could you tell them apart? Could you tell which was mine?'

'I was quite busy trying not to get eaten,' I said apologetically. 'There were three, I think. Two massive great things and a smaller one.' I frowned. *Aunt Grusilla. Pokiss. Lambkin. So where was Jack's?*

'What I can't help wondering,' said Jack slowly, 'is why they *kept* me alive. It was an experiment, to start with, but that was over long ago. They didn't need me any more – and it's not as if my mother ever cared. So why didn't they end it?'

'Aunt Grusilla ended it for Boy,' I told her. 'She chopped down his Halloweed and he just shrivelled away. Uncle Dandelion's plant choked on a pudding. But yours has to be alive, or you wouldn't be here.'

Caramel had been looking more and more bewildered. Now she gave another of her erupting-volcano sneezes.

'Time to get her out of here,' said Jack, as fragments of ceiling rained down on us. 'The Halloweeds can wait.'

As Jack urged her away, Caramel pressed something

into my hand. I felt it crinkle: one of her little paper birds.

'A crane,' Caramel told me. 'For long life – and good luck.'

As I squirmed through the gap beneath the archway, the darkness pressed in around me. Jack had offered me the torch but I'd told her to keep it as I could use the light on my watch. Its glow was green and spooky; I wished I had taken the torch. The squirming was skinning my elbows; soon they were raw and aching.

The passage sloped downhill, Water was coming from somewhere, overtaking me in what started as a trickle then turned into more of a stream. I swallowed a mouthful of it by mistake; it didn't taste too good, so I wriggled with my chin up after that.

When the tunnel forked, I hesitated. Right – or left?

'Martha? Maaaaartha . . .' I was deafened by my own voice bouncing off the tunnel walls.

Da . . . a . . . a . . . an . . . he . . . e . . . e . . . elp . . .

I froze. It was so faint, I wasn't even sure if I'd really heard it. Which fork had it come through? Right? Wrong. Left. *I'm coming, Martha.* I remembered how Caramel's sneezes had rattled the brickwork and didn't dare risk another shout. Dropping one of Jack's coins to mark the turning, hoping the water wouldn't carry it away, I set off again, faster now.

I only noticed the metal grating when it scraped the top of my head. One end of it was hanging loose from the tunnel roof. Up above me, I thought I heard something rustle.

'Martha?'

I squeezed my head and shoulders through the gap into a small, box-like chamber, with stone slabs for walls and a floor of earth. There was no door or windows but a trickle of greenish light dribbled in where the slabs did not quite meet. Here and there the floor was littered with pale, knobbled shapes.

Close to my nose a little snail, striped like a peppermint, was climbing up the side of a flowerpot. It never reached the top – there was a sudden movement, a shiver of leaves and a crunch. The plant in the pot was no higher than a pencil: a single stem with a pair of leaves each side. A young cutting, putting down roots . . . and I knew what had been cut.

I'd seen dead fingers before, dry and dusty, on the Egyptian mummies in the British Museum. This one had been fed and watered; it was greener and less shrivelled. You could still see the knuckle and the nail, poking out of the crumbly brown soil.

An image flashed in my brain: Pokiss's hands, with the extra half a finger missing. She'd planted herself a spare Halloweed. If anything went wrong with her other one – weevils or puddings or Aunt Grusilla losing her temper – this baby was Pokiss's Emergency Backup . . .

Leaves rustled behind me.

'Martha?' Where was she? I tried turning round, but I was wedged too tightly. Something sticky landed on the end of my nose. I wiped it off with the back of my hand. Green. Slimy. Digestive juices . . . My heart gave a sickening kick.

I pulled myself up and on to my knees; the ceiling wasn't high enough to stand. Shuffling awkwardly round, I found myself face to face with another Halloweed – and this one was no baby. Thick-stemmed, with leaves yellow from lack of light, its lower half was coiled like a cobra. Its upper half had Martha wrapped in a deadly hug. Above the rubbery leaf clamped over her nose and mouth, I could see her eyes, round and terrified. I could smell the plant's salami breath as its fleshy lips puckered, ready to start sucking . . .

Desperately, I looked around me for something, anything, to attack it with. Metal glinted on the ground at my feet. I had snatched it up and was slicing the air with it before I realized what it was. A sword. It was the double of the one Robo-Ancestor had been brandishing in my bedroom: the *Dent de Lyon*. This had to be the *other* Tooth of the Lion: the one Sir Lyon de Beaune had taken to his grave.

I knew, now, where I was – and what the pale, knobbly objects scattered around me were. They were all that was left of my ancestors – the bones of Sir Lyon and Lady Clotilda de Beaune ...

The sword was heavy in my hand. *Go on. Use it. What are you waiting for? Chop that thing up – snicker snack – before it can suck all the juices out of Martha.*

But how could I? That Halloweed belonged to somebody. Its sap was somebody's lifeblood. And I thought I knew whose. Jack.

I had two choices: I could let the plant kill Martha – or I could kill Jack.

CHAPTER TWELVE

Sir Lyon had fought the English at the Battle of Hastings with this sword in his hand. My ancestor, the great warrior. It's hard to feel like a great warrior when you are shuffling around on your knees. It's even harder when the last thing you want to do is kill your enemy, because that means killing your friend.

No, the *last* thing I wanted to do was watch my sister get slowly digested by a giant vegetable. I tightened my grip on the hilt.

I'm sorry, Jack. I'm so, so sorry.

Martha jerked and strained in the plant's coils. The smell of rotting meat was suffocating in the cramped tomb. Side-stems came snaking towards me, wrapping themselves around my knees, twining towards my sword arm, tying me down. Even the baby Halloweed was snapping. Martha had green drool running down her face. I couldn't put it off any longer. I raised the Lion's Tooth, taking careful aim with the point, ready to lunge.

Jack, if there was any other way . . .

Quite suddenly, everything changed. In a flurry of tendrils, the Halloweed shrank away, its coils going slack.

'Martha!' I urged, but she was already scrambling free, crawling towards me, wiping the dribble from her eyes. The baby Halloweed was cowering in its pot.

'I never even touched it,' I said. 'What's the matter with them?'

Then I saw the beetle. Nothing special: a little brown beetle with a long snout, making its way along the sword's blade.

'They can't be afraid of *that*,' said Martha.

'Yes, they can,' I told her. 'It's a weevil. Weevils feed on their leaves, then they lay weevil eggs in the roots. The grubs hatch out and start chewing. If they chew up enough root, the plant dies. That's why Aunt Grusilla is so obsessed with unicorns. Unicorn dung keeps the Halloweevils away.'

I stood guard over Martha, sword raised, as she dropped through the grating. The Halloweed stayed pressed against the tomb wall. As I lowered my legs down after her, I caught my breath: in the flickering green light, a skull was grinning at me. Sir Lyon? I laid the Lion's Tooth down beside it.

'Thanks for that,' I said – although it wasn't actually the sword that had saved us. People think insects don't matter. They may be small, but they can make big things happen. In the end, the beetle is mightier than the sword.

Martha was quiet on our way back through the tunnel. Weirdly quiet, for Martha.

'African bat bug,' I said, when I couldn't bear it any longer.

'Bristly rose slug,' said Martha automatically.

'Codling moth.'

'Devil's coach horse.'

We were on Green spoonworms by the time we reached the secret door back into the kitchen.

There was no sign of Jack but, on the other side of the wall, we could hear Aunt Grusilla.

'. . . not at all pleased with you, Pokiss. You didn't catch that unicorn and now you've lost the Heir. I want him found – or I shall string you up from the Hanging

Tree myself. By your feet.'

'Pygmy will be back.' Pokiss sounded sulky. 'Still have smallest. Smallest sssmells,' she added. 'Who will mop it?'

'You,' said Aunt Grusilla. 'Serves you right. Unwrap the horrid little thing. If it's the only one left, we might as well know if it's boy or girl. You know how to tell, I suppose?'

'*Tsss*,' said Pokiss.

'Dan!' whispered Martha, behind me. 'They've got the Grub!'

As I took a quick step forward, there was a sudden TWANG! A yell of pain bubbled up inside me. I clamped my lips together, clenching my fists, trying to keep it in. I tilted the dying glow from my watch down to where blood oozed, dark and sticky, from between steel teeth.

'*Eeew!*' squeaked Martha, wrinkling her nose.

'Did you hear that?' demanded Aunt Grusilla.

'Mousies,' said Pokiss. 'In the walls.'

'Didn't I tell you to put more cheese in the Mechanical Mouse-Mincer?' complained Aunt Grusilla.

Bong! Bong! Bong!

Dizzy with pain, it took me a moment to realize what I was hearing.

Bing-bong! Bing-bong! Bing-bong!

All over the house, clocks were chiming the hour. The last to strike was the grandfather clock in the hall, the elephant of all clocks: *DUNG! DUNG! DUNG! DUNG!*

Jack, I guessed. *She must have gone round winding them all up.*

'Nooooo!' Aunt Grusilla gave a terrible cry. 'I won't have it!' she roared. 'I'll stop them! Pokiss – come with me! Bring the hammer! Quick!'

There were hurried footsteps and the sound of a closing door. Then a wail from the Grub – they'd left it behind. I shone my watch beam around the edges of the secret door. *There!* I'd found what I was looking for: another evil little wooden face. As I reached for its tongue, the door slid back and we stepped through.

'Poor little Grub,' said Martha, scooping it up. 'They put it in a *coffin*!'

I sank into a chair and tried to prise the Mechanical Mouse-Mincer off my toe. Aunt Grusilla and Pokiss would be back any moment, but it was as if my batteries had run out. I was cold and wet, my eyes felt gritty from lack of sleep, and my minced toe was throbbing so hard I could feel it all over my body.

'Did you hear that?' demanded Martha. 'That thing that sounded like thunder? It was my stomach rumbling. I'm *starving*. Do you suppose there's anything you can actually *eat* in that fridge?'

'Careful,' I warned her. 'I wouldn't touch anything Pokiss keeps in her fridge if I were you. It's probably full of bats' brains and pickled toad.'

'It isn't.' Martha was standing in front of the open fridge, just staring. 'Dan, she's got *pizza*. And pasta sauce and yogurt and grapes and . . . and *nice* things.' She looked in the freezer compartment. 'Veggie burgers. And *ice cream*. Do you think she'd notice, if some of her pizza wasn't there?'

'Tricksy little pizza-thief!' said a voice from the doorway.

The pizza box crashed to the floor.

As Pokiss came towards us, I lunged forward on my good foot, making a grab for the goblin.

'Martha – take the Grub! Run!' I yelled, as I tweaked the goblin's tongue to the left. With the Grub in her arms, Martha dived for the door. I tried to follow, but when I put my weight on my injured foot pain ripped through me. The world rocked and blurred; I had to catch hold of the kitchen table to stop myself from falling. I hopped forward, but too late. The door slid shut in my face.

'Dan!' From behind the wall I heard Martha's scream.

I felt Pokiss's cold fingers at the back of my neck. Gripping my collar, she pushed me backwards into a chair. 'All Hallows' Eve,' she hissed in my ear. 'Time for Happy Ever After.' Something flashed in her hand. The snippers.

'No!' I struggled to stand up but Pokiss pushed me back again.

'Bleeding all over Pokiss's clean floor,' she said reproachfully. 'Sssstealing her pizza.'

'I'll buy you more pizza,' I told her. 'Loads – any flavour you like – if you just let us go. Aunt Grusilla will never know. You don't want us here. You don't even like us. Let me go, Pokiss, and you'll never have to see any of us again.'

'*Tsss!* Pokiss can't do that.' Almost, she sounded sorry. 'Must always be a Bone at Daundelyon Hall. Pokiss promised. Pokiss keeps her promises.' She opened up the snippers. 'Sssnicker sssnack . . .'

'Eliza Fishblood.' Jack stood in the doorway.

Something flashed in Pokiss's dishwater eyes. '*Pokisss,*' she hissed. 'Not Eliza. Not any more.'

'You remember her, though, don't you?' said Jack. 'Eliza never meant anybody any harm, did she? She knew about herbs and made her own ointments and helped the sick . . .'

Pokiss's fingers curled into claws. '*Witch*, they called

her. Witch! Witch!'

'They took Eliza away, didn't they?' Jack's voice was quiet and steady. 'They did terrible things to her.'

Pokiss was trembling. 'With their squeezers and stretchers and smashers. Squeeze the witch! Stretch the witch! Smash the witch! Hang the witch!'

'But Eliza didn't hang,' said Jack. 'She made a bargain. In return for her life, she promised my mother that she would be mistress of Daundelyon Hall for ever. To keep that promise, she had to become the witch they said she was. She became—'

'Pokiss*sss*.'

'But Eliza isn't gone. She's still here. And Eliza would never hurt anyone.' Jack tipped back her hat, her one eye holding Pokiss's. 'Eliza,' said Jack, 'would let the boy go.'

I held my breath. The silence stretched out . . .

It was broken by Martha, banging on the wall. 'Dan? *Dan*? Are you all right? I can't make it *open*!'

I could hear the Grub whimpering. They both sounded scared. Pokiss's grip on my wrist had loosened. I pulled my hand free and limped over to the beam, reaching for the goblin's tongue. The door groaned open and Martha tumbled through.

Pokiss hadn't moved. I could hear the soft hiss of her breath, like a punctured football. 'Pokiss knew you'd come back.' She was looking at Jack. 'Flitted away like a moth in the night, but Pokiss knew your Weed would bring you back in the end. Your mother wanted it gone, dead. *Get rid of it*, she said: *snicker-snack*. But Pokiss didn't.' She hesitated, still with that odd, flickering silver light in her eyes. 'Pokiss kept it and hid it in a secret place.'

'Sir Lyon's tomb,' I said. 'I've just met it. It was about to eat Martha.'

'No hard feelings,' said Martha generously. 'It's OK.'

Jack was frowning. 'But . . . why?'

Pokiss wiped her nose on her pyjama sleeve. 'It's yours,' she said. 'It's not for *her* to say what happens to it. Your Weed: your choice . . . *sss*!'

A furious bellow, like a bee-stung bull, made us all jump. '*Pokiss!*' It was Aunt Grusilla. 'Pokiss, where are you? My *hair*! My hair is TICKING!' She burst in through the kitchen door, still in her nightgown and cap, Lambkin pattering at her heels. She was cradling something in her arms; something with a nodding plume of parrot feathers. It took me a moment to realize what it was.

'What a *cheat*!' declared Martha. 'All that patting it and primping it and putting fish in it, and the whole time it was a *wig*!'

Aunt Grusilla ignored her, pushing the pale mound

of her hair at Pokiss. 'Make it STOP!'

We could all hear it. The clock had a very loud tick and didn't say five past one any more.

'Bad luck, Mother,' said Jack. 'Not even you can hold back Time for ever.'

Aunt Grusilla whirled around. 'You! What are *you* doing still alive?' she demanded.

It was at that moment that, in a flash of blue and gold, the parrot came swooping through the doorway, circling the room before landing on a rafter. He cocked his head; his bright yellow eye fixed on Pokiss.

'The parrot feathers!' I realized what he was staring at. The Beak hadn't forgotten his murdered girlfriend – and he'd seen a chance for revenge. 'Pokiss, put down the wig!

But it was too late. The bird was already diving, beak wide open and talons outstretched. '*Pretty Polly!*' he screamed. '*Stuffed! Stufado! Porca, Punschkrapfen, Pasta Puttanesca!*'

Pokiss dropped the wig, and fled.

Lambkin came out from under the kitchen table and pounced, shaking his head and growling as he savaged the mound of hair. As Aunt Grusilla roared at him, lashing out with her foot, there was the clang of a bell and a thunderous knocking on the front doors.

Snatching up her hair and ramming it back on her

head, Aunt Grusilla billowed out of the kitchen. We all crowded after her. A large van was parked outside.

NICKETT & FLOGGITT

said the large letters painted on the side.

IF YOU WANT IT, WE CAN GET IT CHEAP AT HALF THE PRICE

The driver wore jeans and a checked shirt and had a pencil tucked behind his ear. He got out of his van and pushed a clipboard towards us. 'Special delivery for Bone, Daundelyon Hall.'

'Yes!' exclaimed Aunt Grusilla. 'My unicorn!'

'Yeah. Whatever,' said the van man. 'Just sign here.'

A splintering sound came from the back of the removal van and the tip of a horn appeared.

Martha clutched my arm. 'A unicorn! A real one!'

'Maybe,' I said. Something about that horn wasn't right . . .

'Feisty beast,' said the van man. 'It's been crashing about in there all the way up the motorway.' He opened up the back of the van, lowering the ramp then jumping smartly out of the way.

We all held our breath.

Nothing happened. The man gave the side of the van a thwack. From the darkness within came a snort and the clank of a chain. The next moment something large, wrinkled and furious came charging down the ramp. We all took a step backwards. The unicorn galumphed as far as it could before reaching the end of its chain. Pulled up short, it stood pawing the ground and swinging its head. It looked about as friendly – or mythical – as an armoured tank.

'That is *not* what I ordered,' said Aunt Grusilla. 'Do I look stupid? I ordered a unicorn. That is a rhinoceros.'

The van man looked at his clipboard. 'Not what it says here. Monoceros Rarissimus. Signature required on receipt.'

'It's sweet,' said Martha. 'Can I stroke it?'

'It's stolen,' I said. 'It's an Indian rhinoceros and it was stolen from a wildlife park. I saw it in the paper when we were on the train, coming here.'

'I wouldn't know anything about that.' The van man seemed in a hurry to be gone. 'I just make the deliveries.'

'There's been a mistake.' Aunt Grusilla glared at the Monoceros Rarissimus. 'Where's Pokiss?'

'There.' Jack pointed.

Midnight burst out of the stable block in a hailstorm of hooves. He reared up at sight of the Monoceros, then took off at a gallop, heading for the drawbridge. Pokiss was crouched low over his neck, her cobweb hair streaming out from under her bobble hat. Behind her, one to each side, like an escort of small black fighter planes, flew a pair of crows.

'Pokiss, where are you *going*?' Aunt Grusilla was trembling with rage, like milk about to boil. 'You made a promise, remember? I saved your life. That makes you mine. For ever.'

'Nothing really lasts for ever,' said Jack. 'Pokiss did everything you asked of her, for several lifetimes. She deserves a holiday. I don't think she'll be back.'

I didn't think so, either. I'd seen what Pokiss was carrying, clutched under her arm. Her *grimoire* and a flowerpot. I was pretty sure I knew what was growing in that pot. One green finger.

The van man had closed up the back of his van. Before he got back in his cab, he handed the end of the Monoceros's chain to Martha.

'Martha, you've caught a unicorn!' I said. 'You must be a virtuous maiden after all. . .'

'I don't want to be a virtuous maiden,' Martha objected. 'I want to be a witch.'

'Wait!' commanded Aunt Grusilla. 'I will *not* be fobbed off with that ugly beast when I *specifically* ordered a unicorn.'

Jack shrugged. 'Unicorn. Monoceros. It means the

same thing. One horn. Things don't always turn out quite the way you expect. Anyway, it's too late now.'

The key was already in the ignition. The van man waved a hand through the cab window, then he was gone, into the cloud of dust kicked up by Midnight's hooves. He made it through the portcullis just in time. It came crashing down after him, making us all jump and missing the back of the van by centimetres.

The Monoceros was clearly having a bad day. Towing Martha behind her, she was taking out her bad temper on a bush cut into the shape of a peacock. She ripped at it with her horn, then trampled it flat. Finally, just to make sure, she sat on it.

'She's so sweet,' said Martha fondly. 'I shall call her Buttercup. Can't we take this horrid chain off? It's hurting her neck and making her sad.'

'Better keep it on until she's settled down,' advised Jack. Taking the chain from Martha, she looped it around the stone unicorn that guarded one side of the Hall's doors. Pulling it tight, Jack glanced around her, frowning. 'Where's my mother?'

While we were admiring Buttercup, Aunt Grusilla had disappeared.

'The Glass House!' I suddenly had a bad feeling. I met Jack's one eye and knew she had it too.

The Glass House door was open. Inside, Aunt Grusilla was busy with the snippers. Leaf by leaf, stalk by stalk, tendril by tendril, she was hacking one of the Halloweeds into little pieces.

'That's the end of *her*!' she crowed, seeing our shocked faces. 'Hocus pocus, no more Pokiss!' As she brandished the snippers, the Halloweeds on either side of her flinched and trembled. Aunt Grusilla pointed the snapping blades at Jack. '*You* shouldn't be here – and very soon you won't be. It's long past your deathtime, miss! Pokiss and her sneaky lies – she should have finished you off long ago. Better late than never – and I know where that Halloweed of yours is hiding . . .'

With a jolt of fear, I saw that the end slab of Sir Lyon and Lady Clotilda's tomb had been pushed to one side. *Pokiss was here to fetch her plant. She must have left it open . . .*

Snippers in one hand, Aunt Grusilla held up a string of sausages in the other. The Halloweeds dribbled at the sight of them, writhing and snapping. Aunt Grusilla jabbed at them with the snippers and they drew back. Lambkin had crept out from behind a gravestone and was begging, up on his back legs. Aunt Grusilla kicked him away.

'Come out, my little shrinking violet! Come out, come out, wherever you are!' she coaxed, dangling the sausages in front of the open tomb.

Nothing happened.

'Lovely juicy sausages!' wheedled Aunt Grusilla, stroking their smooth pinkness. 'Just for you . . .'

Slowly green tendrils came creeping out. They swayed this way and that, tasting the air, then began pulling towards the sausages.

'Come on, little Cabbage,' called Aunt Grusilla. 'Come to Mother . . .'

Jack's Halloweed burst out into the light, slime-strings of drool hanging from its jaws. Aunt Grusilla stepped backwards, dangling the sausages just out of reach. With her other hand, she took a grip on the snippers.

'No!' I said, as she lifted them. 'Don't!'

Aunt Grusilla was laughing. 'Say goodbye, dearest daughter!'

'Mother, please.' Jack was standing beside me, stiff and pale. 'Give me a little time. A day. An hour . . .'

'Haven't I given you enough time already?' snapped Aunt Grusilla. 'You owe me three hundred years and a great deal of potting compost! If you want more, give me the boy. He is the Heir and I *shall* have his finger!'

'No,' said Jack.

'Suit yourself,' said Aunt Grusilla, opening the snippers.

'Wait!' I took a step forward. 'You can have my finger. Take it – and leave Jack alone.'

'Dan, no!' Martha tried to pull me back, but I shook her off.

'Dan, you don't have to do this.' Jack's voice was urgent.

I just shook my head and kept on going, towards Aunt Grusilla and her snippers. I could hear my heart, pounding in my ears. One finger. It wasn't that big a price to pay . . . How many people get the chance to live for ever? The world had changed since Jack ran away from the Hall. Back then, there'd been no electricity; no cars or planes or computers. How different would it be in another three hundred years? Full of robots and space buses and flying houses and probably a load of other things nobody had even thought of yet. Did I want to miss all that?

Right now, I didn't much care. What mattered was stopping Aunt Grusilla: I wasn't going to let her kill Jack.

It was Lambkin's frantic barking that gave the first warning. Then we all felt it. The Glass House walls were vibrating. The ground began to shake. Jack glanced over her shoulder, and let out a shout.

'Dan, Martha! Get out of the way!'

Buttercup had broken her chain. The loose end came trailing after her as she galumphed at top speed towards the Glass House. She just kept on coming, like an asteroid hurtling through space.

We leapt for safety – all except for Aunt Grusilla. Jack's Halloweed had slithered back into Sir Lyon's tomb. Aunt Grusilla was trying to grab it back.

'Come out of there,' she told it furiously. 'You won't escape me, you great creeping cucumber! I shall get the weedkiller: you'll wither away . . .'

In spite of everything, I thought somebody ought to tell her. 'Aunt Grusilla – watch out!'

Some people never listen.

A group of rhinoceroses is called a *crash*. As Buttercup burst through the Glass House doors, you could see why. Glass tinkled, terracotta pots smashed, stems snapped, hanging baskets swung in wild circles, gravestones toppled. Aunt Grusilla was bending over, her arms inside the tomb, making wild stabs with the snippers. Her wide behind was directly in Buttercup's path . . .

Rhinoceroses have poor eyesight. Their brakes aren't good either. As Buttercup kept going, head down, her long horn passed straight through Aunt Grusilla's skirts and spiked the mound of her wig. Blinded by folds of flapping nightgown, the rhinoceros tossed her head upwards, trying to free herself. On she dashed, with the wig impaled on her horn and Aunt Grusilla, bald as an egg and bellowing, riding on her nose. It seemed as if she would charge right through the Glass House and out the other side but, weighed down by a load of aunt, she suddenly ran out of steam. Stopping in her tracks, she rubbed her head against a gravestone, trying to scrape off her unwanted passenger.

Cautiously we came out of our hiding places. Aunt Grusilla had tumbled off Buttercup. Wrenching what was left of her wig off the horn, she stuck it back on her head. She didn't seem to be hurt, just purple with rage.

'She was lucky it was just her wig,' said Martha. 'She could have had a hole stuck through her like a doughnut.'

'I'm not so sure about the luck,' I said. 'Look at her Halloweed.'

While Aunt Grusilla was trying to drag Jack's plant out of the tomb, her own Halloweed had come snaking behind her, following the smell of sausages. Buttercup had trampled right over its stem. Mangled and bruised, oozing sap, it lay twitching on the ground.

We all looked at Aunt Grusilla.

'*Nooooooo!*'

Rushing to the side of the dying plant, she dropped to her knees, trying to straighten bent stalks and fluff up wilting leaves.

'No, no, my blossom, my flower, my precious petal.' Was it just the morning light coming through the glass roof – the first sunny day in weeks – or was her skin turning a curious shade of pale green?

'We shall make you better,' crooned Aunt Grusilla. 'We shall feed you.' She tried to cram the sausages into its jaws, but the Halloweed was past being greedy and lay quite limp.

Something was definitely happening to Aunt Grusilla...

She was losing her shape, blurring at the edges. It was a bit like watching candlewax melt.

'It's not over, my precious blossom,' she crooned.

But you could see that it was. Leaves rustled as Jack's Halloweed came twining out of its tomb to join Lambkin's. Stems swayed, tendrils curled and flexed as they reared up on either side of Aunt Grusilla.

Then they swooped.

It didn't last long. I know that because I closed my eyes; when I opened them again, it was all over. There was nothing to see, except a few wisps of hair.

Nobody spoke.

Except the parrot, fluffing his feathers on the head of a grieving angel.

'*Che cavolo!*' it cackled. '*Buon appetito!* Dish of the day – stuffed cabbage and bully beef!'

CHAPTER
THIRTEEN

It was four days later when the letter came, I was leading the Monoceros Rarissimus over the drawbridge for her morning walk. Martha sat on her back, wearing Boy's top hat with the parrot perched on top of it.

The rain had cleared after what Martha called Buttercup Day, when Pokiss and Aunt Grusilla had gone their separate ways, and the sun had come out. We spent our time in the woods, or paddling the *Biscuit* around the moat. At night we curled in patchwork hammocks on the *Goose* or camped on deck, under the stars.

As the post van braked, I limped to a halt. My foot

still hurt. When Jack had seen my Mechanically-Minced toe, she had saddled Death, put me up in front of her and ridden to the nearest hospital. The car park attendant had told us off for parking Death in the hospital car park, even though we'd stuck a ticket on his neck, but when he saw all the blood, he'd changed his mind and gone to get me a wheelchair. The tip of my toe had come right off. The doctor said that if I'd picked it up and got there sooner, they could have stitched it back on for me. I wasn't that bothered. I still had ten fingers; I could spare half a toe.

'What?' said Martha, when she saw the postman staring.

'Master D. Bone? Miss M. Bone? Letter for you.'

I took the envelope he was holding out. The stamps were brightly coloured and foreign. Somebody had crossed out the address with thick black lines, scrawling *Daundelyon Hall, Witches' Cross* in its place, but you could still make out what it said:

32 Shakespeare Road.

I knew that handwriting. For a moment, I forgot to breathe.

As the postman reversed down the lane, I slit open the envelope, unfolding the thin sheet of blue paper. There was a row of *xxxxxx* scribbled on the back and a doodled picture of a beetle. My heart was beating so hard, I had to hold on to Buttercup's horn to steady myself.

I read it aloud: '*Dearest Dan and Martha, I hope you're both well and happy, and looking after the Grub. Dad and I have been having rather an exciting time in the rainforest. We set off with another couple, Mr and Mrs Goode, who have been here before and offered to be our guides. We even thought we had found the Greater-Spotted Giant Purple One-Horned Dung Beetle! (It turned out to be the Lesser-Spotted sort, which was disappointing, but then a very rare spider got into our tent and bit your father, so that cheered us up.)*

'*Everything was going fine until the Goodes turned out to be not very nice people. They tied us to a tree and ran off with everything we had – even Dad's SpongeBob SquarePants watch!*'

I stopped, remembering the last time I'd seen that watch – in the photograph Mr Stilton had shown us, that last day at school. The clasped, severed hands: no bodies, no faces to prove whom they had *really* belonged to . . .

'Go on,' said Martha, impatient.

'*There we were, tied up in the middle of nowhere for two whole days! We were a tiny bit worried – we had heard that the local people were cannibals – but the ones who rescued us turned out to be charming. They took us back to meet the rest of the tribe. They had had a big feast the night before and gave us some of the leftovers. (We couldn't work out exactly what it was. They called it Long Pig, but I thought it tasted more like roast chicken.)*

'We never did find out what happened to Mr and Mrs Goode.

'Still no sign of that pesky G-S.G.P.O-H.D.B., I'm afraid, but never mind.'

'The What?' asked Martha.

'Greater-Spotted Giant Purple One-Horned Dung Beetle,' I told her. 'Don't interrupt – this is the important bit.'

'By the time you get this, we'll be on our way home. You three are more important than any beetle and I can't wait to see you all again and give you a hug. Kiss the Grub from me, and say hello to Caramel. Lots of love, Mum xxx

'P.S. Dad has drawn you some pictures of the G-S.G.P.O-H.D.B.'

'Gorgonzola Guacamole Gugelhupf!' said Martha. (She'd been taking lessons from the parrot.) She gave a little bounce. 'Dan, it was my *spell*. It worked – I brought them back!'

'Mmm,' I said, looking back at the letter. '*Or* the whole thing was just a mistake . . .'

Martha ignored that. 'We have to go,' she said. If they

get home and we're not there, they won't know where we are. They'll fuss.' She paused. 'Can you take a rhinoceros on a train?'

'Buttercup doesn't belong to us,' I reminded her. 'She belongs at the wildlife park. She probably wants to go home as much as you do.'

'I do want to,' agreed Martha, with a sigh. 'Only . . . I may never get to ride a rhinoceros again.'

'And there's Jack,' I said. 'We'd better go and tell her.' I knew how Martha felt. I'd longed to go home, and see Mum and Dad again, more than anything else in the world. Now it was going to happen – and all I could think of was what we had to leave behind. 'She'll be on the *Goose*. Come on.'

We found Jack polishing the ship's wheel. Lambkin-Wolfsnarl was with her, curled up asleep on a scrap of old sailcloth, twitching as he dreamed.

'I miss the old days,' she admitted, stroking beeswax into the wooden spokes. 'All that sky and sea, and nothing in between. Sometimes I think: just one last voyage . . . But the *Goose* is too old to fly any more.'

She read our letter, then folded it up and handed it back. 'You'll be leaving, then.'

'Come with us,' I said. 'Please. Come and live with us. Mum and Dad won't mind.'

'You can bring the Beak and Barnacle and Lambkin-Wolfsnarl,' added Martha. 'You belong with us. We're your family.'

Jack had gone back to polishing her spokes. 'We should have a party,' she said without looking up. 'A Parting Party.'

'It's the fifth of November tomorrow,' I said. 'That means . . .'

Martha clapped her hands. 'It's Bonfire Night!'

The next day, Caramel brushed the hay off her bike and roared across the drawbridge, with Jack riding pillion behind her. They came back with bursting saddlebags and a cloud of smiley-faced helium balloons tied to the number plate.

'Schnitzel!' said the parrot, very much alarmed, and spent the rest of the afternoon up a tree.

'In some parts of the world,' said Jack, 'they invite the dead to parties. They wake them up and dance with them. I like that.' She looked thoughtfully towards the Glass House where Boy had the peace and quiet he'd wanted at last. Aunt Grusilla, who didn't take up much space any more, was sharing a grave with Uncle Dandelion.

'I get cross when people wake me up,' objected Martha. 'Do we really want a load of cross dead people hanging about?'

'We'll let them lie,' said Jack, rather to my relief. I had already got closer to Sir Lyon and Lady Clotilda than I'd have chosen to. 'They can come if they feel like it.'

I don't know if any ghosts came floating out of the Glass House that night. If they did, I hope they enjoyed themselves. Jack had spent the afternoon chopping up coffins. By the time the sun went down, we had heaped the wood into one huge pile in the centre of the courtyard. Once it was lit, the flames flickered and danced, leaping upwards to the inky sky. Fairy lights glittered in Boy's topiary bushes, over the arch of the gatehouse and along the edges of the draw-bridge. The lion and the unicorn guarding the front doors wore garlands of dandelion flowers around their necks, and Martha had given all the suits of armour a party hat and a balloon.

Caramel had draped a cloth over Buttercup's broad back and turned her into a walking table. She wandered about as she pleased and everyone helped themselves to sandwiches and handfuls of crisps as she passed, while jugs of lemonade and purple fruit punch cooled in an ice-filled coffin.

As I reached out for a chicken leg, the rhinoceros tossed her head, her horn sparkling.

I looked at Martha, who was toasting a marshmallow. 'Is Buttercup wearing Aunt Grusilla's diamonds?'

Martha giggled. 'She looks so much prettier in them than Aunt Gruesome did, don't you think?'

Lambkin-Wolfsnarl was in a pearl tiara; Martha had tried slipping an emerald bracelet over the parrot's head but he had yanked it off, with a fierce foot, and flung it on the floor.

'*Nacho Princessatarta!*' he had screeched at Martha, flapping his wings at her. '*Polpettine! Albondigas! Frikadeller! Gehaktballen!*'

'What's he saying?' demanded Martha, backing away.

'Meatballs,' translated Jack, apologetically. 'Ignore him, Martha. He has shocking manners.'

We bobbed for apples, and ate doughnuts with no hands and played Pin-the-Wart-on-the-Witch.

'How far do you think Pokiss got,' wondered Martha, 'before Aunt Gruesome chopped her down?'

Midnight had come trotting home, wet, cold and riderless, when the grisly events in the Glass House were all over — we had to wind up the portcullis on creaking, rusty chains to let him in. Everyone thought Pokiss was gone for good: nothing left but a scattering of bones by the roadside somewhere.

I knew better.

'She's not dead,' I said. 'Some people keep spare house keys, or spare spectacles. Pokiss kept a spare Halloweed. She had two fingers missing, didn't you see?'

Martha frowned. 'Why would she want to cut off another one?'

'She knew what might happen if my mother lost her temper,' guessed Jack. 'Or maybe it was because of the weevils ...'

We had got rid of the Halloweevils. Caramel had ridden her bike to the nearest garden centre and come back with a spray can of Weevil-Off Special Formula and a bottle of something called BOOM-GRO.

'My Uncle Ferdy grows prize marrows,' she explained. 'He feeds them on this stuff and they grow twice as big as anybody else's. You don't need actual blood and bones.'

'I'm glad Pokiss is still alive,' decided Jack. 'She deserves a second chance.'

I agreed, but I couldn't help wondering who it was out there, with her crows and her plant pot and her grimoire. If it was Eliza, then I wished her luck. If it was Pokiss ... I shivered.

Fireworks took our minds off lost witches, good or bad. The darkness exploded into clouds of sparkles and spangles, spitting and glittering, as Jack set them off on the drawbridge. (The animals, including Buttercup, were all safely shut up in the Hall, in case the bangs and flashes upset them. A startled rhinoceros is never the best sort.)

As stars showered down over Daundelyon Hall, the smell of gunpowder hung in the air.

'It takes me back,' said Jack, breathing it in. 'Cannonballs and battles at sea.' She tipped her head back, watching a flash of light spiral, screaming, up into the night sky. 'What do you suppose is up there? Heaven? Aliens? Or just lots of nothing?'

Nobody answered, because nobody knew.

'I wouldn't mind finding out,' said Jack. 'One last adventure . . .'

'I don't want it to end,' said Martha, when the last sparkler had fizzled out. 'I want it to go on and on and on being this evening.'

'There's been enough holding back Time,' said Jack. 'Your future's waiting for you, Martha.'

'But I don't know what's in it,' complained Martha. 'Why can't the future be like television, when they say *Coming up next* . . . and show you all the best bits before they happen?'

'Supposing they showed you something horrible?' I argued. 'You'd wouldn't know when it was coming;

you'd be waiting and waiting . . .'

Martha shook her head, obstinate. 'I'd still want to know.'

'I met a fortune-teller once,' said Jack. 'Her name was Crystal Lil. It was after I lost my eye.'

'Did you lose it in a fight?' Martha wanted to know.

'No,' said Jack. 'It was one starry night on the Spanish Main. A pirate named Dead-Eye Dick balanced a pomegranate on my head and bet me his wooden leg that he could split it with an arrow, blindfold, at twenty paces. He lost the bet and I lost my eye, although I did gain a leg. It came in very useful for games of French cricket on deck when we were becalmed. The point is, Crystal Lil said it was a shame for a handsome lad with a fine moustache to be missing an eye – she was a little short-sighted – so she gave me this.'

I saw her hand go up to her eyepatch, then she was holding out her hand. On her palm rolled something like a large marble, the moon shining in its mirrored surface.

I'd just taken a sip of lemonade. Now it went the wrong way, fizzing up my nose, making me sneeze.

'Not terribly good manners to snort lemonade all over people's eyes,' said Jack, wiping it on her sleeve.

Martha stared at it, fascinated. 'You can't actually *see*

with it, though. Can you?'

'That depends,' said Jack. 'If you're brave enough, take a look. Catch!'

We all jumped, but it was Martha who caught it and held it in her cupped hands.

'What do you see?' asked Jack.

'Nothing.' Martha sounded disappointed. 'Just me. My reflection.'

'That's where it all begins – with the person you are,' said Jack. 'The future doesn't just *happen*. You have to make it. Look harder.'

'I'm looking so hard it *hurts*,' complained Martha. 'All I can see is— Oh!'

'What?' Caramel and I crowded around her. 'What is it?'

'Mum!' Martha gave a little bounce and almost dropped the eyeball. 'And Dad!'

'Let me see!' I reached out, but she held the eye away from me. 'Wait. I can see Caramel. Who's that man?' Martha frowned. 'It's that man on the train – the hairy ginger person with the tarantula tattoo.'

'Oh!' Caramel had gone pink-ish. 'His name was Keith. I may have given him my phone number,' she admitted.

'You don't even *know* him!' said Martha, shocked. She gave the eye a shake. 'He won't go away!' she complained. 'You're standing next to him, Caramel, wearing a *veil* and carrying a load of old flowers. And there's Mum again, in a silly hat – and why am I wearing a *dress*? I hate dresses . . . oh, *meatballs*!' She gave Caramel a stern look. 'I'm your *bridesmaid*!'

Caramel gave a sort of whimpery squeak. 'My legs have gone wobbly,' she muttered and sat down, hard, on the stairs.

'The future can be difficult to swallow – too much, too fast,' warned Jack. She held out her hand, but Martha passed the eye to me instead. 'What do *you* see, Dan?'

The eye was smooth and cold against my skin. I wasn't expecting to see anything except my own reflection, but then the ball's surface shivered like rippling water.

'Can you see them? Mum and Dad?' Martha was jostling me, trying to see too. I shook her off, lifting the ball out of her reach, not taking my eyes off it, not even daring to blink, in case what I'd seen disappeared.

There they were: small and far off, but Mum and Dad just as I remembered them. Although . . . as I watched, something was happening. Dad's hair was slipping backwards off his head; Mum was greyer now, with lines on her face. They seemed to shrink and hunch up – since when had Mum had all those wrinkles, and why was Dad walking with a stick? Their faces shimmered and broke up; now it was Martha, but the wrong Martha – older than me, with lipstick on, then with silver hair and spectacles. And who was that tall, serious person – surely that couldn't be the *Grub*?

And what about me? Where was I? I turned the ball this way and that, searching. *There.* Staring back at me: ordinary me, the same as always.

My heart gave a sudden kick; I caught my breath.

I'd seen what was behind my reflection. Twining around my shoulders, nuzzling my ear, the sap bubbling from its fleshy cabbage jaws . . .

A Halloweed.

I spun round.

'Dan? What's the matter?' Martha was staring at me. 'You've gone all weird-looking.'

My hand was shaking. The eye fell from my hand and skittered across the floor. Lambkin-Wolfsnarl chased after it but Jack stopped it with the toe of her boot and picked it up, dropping it in her pocket.

'I saw a Halloweed . . . right here, behind me . . .'

'Stupid,' said Martha kindly. 'They're tucked up in the Glass House. You know they are.'

'The future's all right in its place,' said Jack, giving me a sideways look out of her one good eye. 'When it comes too close – that's when it gets scary.'

I knew what she meant: watching Mum and Dad and Martha and the Grub grow old had scared me more than a Halloweed ever could. But the plant I'd seen hadn't wanted to hurt me, I was sure of it. But *why not*? It was almost as if we belonged together, it and I.

I glanced down at my fingers: ten of them, all where they should be. So, apart from the usual things, like asteroids and super-volcanoes and the sun turning into a red dwarf and nostril hair and going bald, there was nothing to worry about. *Was there?*

'Have you looked in it, Jack?' asked Martha. 'It's *your* eye. What did you see?'

Jack shrugged. 'There's such a thing as having too much Future. It's all a bit of a blur. I saw you two in it once. A long time ago – I don't suppose your grandparents were even born.'

We stared at her. 'Did you know who we were?' I asked.

Jack hunched up a shoulder. 'When I was little – before the Halloweeds – I used to dream about what it would be like to have a brother or a sister. I reckoned that was all you were: imaginary. *Hey!*' She pulled away from Martha's pinch. 'What was that for?'

'Just proving it,' said Martha. 'I am *not* imaginary.'

CHAPTER FOURTEEN

For the first time since Buttercup Day, we slept at the Hall that night.

I dreamed. In my dream, I woke up to find Pokiss standing over me, staring down at me with strange, silvery eyes. I couldn't move, or scream, the way you can't in dreams. All I could do was lie there.

Lion-toothed, sharp of claw,
Bones rule, ever more.
Here lives and breathes a true-born Bone,
Or these walls crumble, stone by stone.

As her lips moved, the words echoed around my head. When I woke up properly, I was twitchy and sweating.

I slept with the lamp on, after that.

When I woke again, I could tell by the light that it was very early morning.

We're going home today, I thought. I stood by the window, looking out over the moat as the milky sky turned morning-fresh blue. The sound of creaking wheels made me glance down into the courtyard. Jack was down there, with Lambkin-Wolfsnarl at her heels. She was pushing a wheelbarrow full of . . .

I leant further out of the window, staring.

Halloweeds.

Tugging on jeans and a T-shirt, I ran downstairs. Buttercup was asleep at the foot of the stairs. Jumping over her, I nearly landed in a large pile of rhinoceros dung. Swerving away from it, I noticed the beetle.

It was large-ish, purple-ish and spotty-ish and it was very busy rolling a little lump of rhinoceros poo into a ball. A dung beetle. And not just any old dung beetle. A Greater-Spotted Giant Purple One-Horned Dung Beetle! I'd seen the pictures – I was sure of it. Mum and Dad had gone all the way to the rainforest, when all they actually needed to do was drive down the motorway to the wildlife park . . .

I caught up with Jack down by the river. The Halloweeds were writhing and snapping at flies as she loaded them on to the *Biscuit*.

'What are you doing?' I asked.

Jack hunched one shoulder. Her hat was tipped low over her nose. 'Goodbyes are better said before breakfast. Or not at all.'

'But our train doesn't go until after lunch,' I reminded her. 'We're not leaving for ages yet.'

'No,' said Jack, 'but I am.'

'Where are you going?'

'Who knows?' said Jack. 'Until I get there. One last adventure.'

'You said we could have adventures together,' I reminded her.

'You have Martha to look after,' said Jack. 'And the Grub.'

'They'll be all right,' I said. 'They won't need me once Mum and Dad are home.'

Jack shook her head. 'They do need you,' she said. 'And you need them. You should be with the people you love while you can. A lifetime is never as long as you think.'

'Why do you want to take *them*?' I looked at the Halloweeds. They seemed to be enjoying their outing from the Glass House. Trailing its tendrils in the water, Jack's dived suddenly, coming up with a fish in its jaws. 'I can look after them for you,' I offered – although keeping flesh-eating Cabbages at 32 Shakespeare Road was likely to have its awkward moments. 'I won't let anything happen to them.'

'Something has to happen to them, in the end,' said Jack. 'Nothing lasts for ever. That's not how it works.'

A package on the floor of the *Biscuit* had caught my eye. Between the folds of a length of sailcloth, I caught the glint of metal. I leant over and pulled the cloth away. The *Dent de Lyon*.

'You don't mind, do you?' asked Jack. 'You won't need it.' She pushed back her hat and smiled. 'You're strong enough and sharp enough without it. On the inside, where it counts.'

I looked at the Halloweeds' fleshy stems. That blade would slice through them like butter. And then what? I thought of Boy and Uncle Dandelion, and of what had happened to Aunt Grusilla. A bad feeling was uncurling inside me. 'Jack, what are you going to do?'

'Nothing,' said Jack. 'Yet. One day, when the Time is right. I just want to know that it's up to me – that I have the choice. That's what I came back for.'

'Don't go,' I begged. 'Come with us. You belong with us.'

But Jack shook her head. 'I belong to the past,' she said. 'Not the future. It's better to keep things in order. Look after the Beak for me, won't you? The Barnacle is in the stables – he'll want to stay with the horses.' The little white donkey had made firm friends with Death.

I nodded. 'The girl from the farm is coming for them after breakfast. And the people from the wildlife park are coming for Buttercup. Everybody's going,' I complained. 'What will happen to the Hall? It will be empty. No *true-born Bone*. No anybody.'

I thought I knew the answer. Daundelyon Hall would crumble away, left to the weevils and the woodworm and the Deathwatch beetle. The Glass House would splinter and fall while a thousand years of Bones slept, unbothered, underneath . . .

'Life's like the river,' said Jack. 'It can't stay still, has to keep moving. This is for you, Dan. Something to remember me by.'

I thought for a moment that she had passed me a dead mouse, then I realized it was her moustache.

'I knew there was something different about you.' I stared at her, then down at the soft thing in my hand. 'Your moustache! It suits you. Not having one, I mean.'

Jack shrugged. 'I don't need it any more. Keep it; it may come in useful one day. And there's this. Here, take it.'

A little *Flying Goose*: the one I had seen in her cabin, carved out of wood.

'It's a different flag,' I said. Below the smiling skull was not just one bone, but three.

Jack nodded. 'You, Martha and the Grub. Say goodbye to them all for me, Dan.'

Jack climbed on board, whistling to Lambkin-Wolfsnarl who jumped in after her, tail waving. As she picked up the paddle, I felt a sudden urge to rush forward and jump in too. *I'm coming with you. Wait for me . . .* I felt the words rise up in my throat but then I thought of Martha, waking up and finding me gone, and I knew I couldn't do it . . .

Casting off from the bank, Jack raised her hand in a final, four-fingered salute. As the current caught it, the *Biscuit* bobbed merrily down-river, growing smaller and smaller. All I could see of Jack now was her hat, tipped over her nose, as the Halloweeds twined around her. Then the river curved around the edge of the Deepness and there was nothing left to see at all.

The train wasn't crowded; we had a table all to ourselves. The parrot, shut up in a cat basket, was muttering darkly to himself about *devilled kidneys* and *death by chocolate*. Martha's dinosaurs were packed in her suitcase. Instead, she had a second basket on her lap. Green eyes gleamed through the wickerwork: it was the grey cat.

'Isn't it funny?' said Martha, as we pulled out of Witches' Cross station. 'When we arrived, everything was All Wrong. Now it's All Right. Except for Jack leaving, of course. We can all start living happily ever after.'

'Ever after is a long time,' I said.

The thought of *ever after* had been niggling at me since I'd drawn my curtains that morning and seen what was on my window sill: a small terracotta pot, filled with soil. In the middle of it, something green, just beginning to sprout: a slender shoot poking up out of something that looked like a shrivelled green bean.

It wasn't a bean.

It was the tip of my toe.

It hadn't been a dream, after all. Pokiss – or Eliza – had been at Daundelyon Hall last night; I had my very own Halloweed. How many days was it since I'd grown any older? Did I feel any different? I wasn't sure. And what was I going to do about it? I had time to make up my mind. Mum was always complaining I grew out of my clothes too fast. She'd be pleased that I'd slowed down; it would take her a while to notice that I'd stopped altogether. If it was Pokiss who took my toe, I reckoned it was Eliza Fishblood, the girl from long ago, who gave it back. Eliza, who knew what Jack knew: it's having the choice that matters.

Gazing out of the window as trees and hedges and fields full of cows flashed past, I considered my options.

The tiny cabbage-thing in my backpack was delicate, only just alive.

I could care for it, give it what it needed, keep it safe from weevils – and stay eleven for ever.

Or I could ignore it, stamp on it, feed it weedkiller, let it die – and grow up.

The future was up to me. All I had to do was choose.

With a huge thank you to the lovely (and patient!) team at Chicken House, especially Rachel L and Kesia, who rescued me when I got lost in the Deepness.